The Doomsday Marshal
and the Comancheros

The Doomsday Marshal
and the Comancheros

RAY HOGAN

A DOUBLE D WESTERN
DOUBLEDAY
NEW YORK   LONDON   TORONTO   SYDNEY   AUCKLAND

A Double D Western
PUBLISHED BY DOUBLEDAY
a division of Bantam Doubleday Dell Publishing Group, Inc.
666 Fifth Avenue, New York, New York 10103

A DOUBLE D WESTERN, DOUBLEDAY, and the portrayal of the letters DD
are trademarks of Doubleday, a division of Bantam Doubleday Dell
Publishing Group, Inc.

Library of Congress Cataloging-in-Publication Data
Hogan, Ray, 1908–
The Doomsday marshal and the Comancheros/Ray Hogan.—1st ed.
p.   cm.—(A Double D Western)
1. Comanche Indians—Fiction.   I. Title.
PS3558.03473D634   1990
813'.54—dc20   89-33826
CIP

ISBN 0-385-26296-5
Copyright © 1990 by Ray Hogan
All Rights Reserved
Printed in the United States of America
First Edition
January 1990
OG

For my wife—Lois

*The Doomsday Marshal
and the Comancheros*

CHAPTER 1

John Rye considered his prisoner narrowly. Hoyt was slightly ahead of him astride the bay gelding the lawman had rented in Santa Fe for him to ride to El Paso. There, the squat, red-haired outlaw with four killings to his credit was to be turned over to the border town's marshal.

Rye glanced about. They were three, perhaps four, miles from the settlement. To their left were the ragged foothills of the Franklin Mountains; to the right—the west—lay a narrow, brushy strip of land on the yonder side of which flowed southward in muddy sluggishness, the Rio Grande.

"If you're getting a notion to make a run for it," the famed Doomsday Marshal said quietly, "forget it. I'll blow your damned head off before you've gone ten feet."

"That'd be better than hanging," Hoyt said without looking around. "Don't much fancy dying, but if I'm due I sure don't like the idea of it being at the end of a rope."

"Those men you shot down didn't fancy it either," the lawman said, "but you didn't give them a choice."

"They were ragging me. Was no reason for them to be doing it."

"Still gave you no call to gun them down."

Hoyt settled back in his saddle. He half turned, sharp features set; small, dark eyes filled with bitterness.

"What the hell do you know about what I've had to put up with all my life? You're lucky. You're a tall man, not a shorty like me."

Rye shrugged. "Something neither one of us had anything to do with," he said, looking upward. "All we can do about it is make the best of it."

Several buzzards were circling slowly overhead. Wings spread, they appeared motionless against the clean, startling blue sky.

"I reckon you can say that real easy," Hoyt grumbled, shifting again in the saddle. "How far are we from El Paso?"

"Not far. See that smoke ahead? That'll be it."

Rye allowed his hand to fall away from the butt of the .45 Colt revolver he carried. Maybe Hoyt wasn't going to be a fool and try to escape after all, but the marshal was a man who took nothing for granted; he'd still keep a close watch on the outlaw.

He had taken charge of Scrub Hoyt in the old New Mexico capital of Santa Fe two weeks ago, acting on orders from the chief marshal in Washington. The outlaw had broken out of a Texas jail where he was awaiting execution for murder, only to be captured by the sheriff up in Taos county who in turn handed him over to the law officials in Santa Fe.

Two days before the Santa Fe sheriff planned to conduct the outlaw to El Paso he became involved in an argument with several drunks in Maria Cristina's saloon and was knifed several times. None of his wounds were mortal, but he was compelled to forget the three-hundred-fifty-mile ride to El Paso with a dangerous criminal in his care.

Rye, laying over in Santa Fe for a few days while en route from Arizona where he had delivered a prisoner to the jail in Prescott, was on his way to Wichita. Word from the chief marshal—who somehow knew he would be in the old capital—awaited him there. He was directed to take charge of Hoyt and conduct him to El Paso.

It didn't matter to Rye that his plans were interrupted. His profession was the law—the apprehension of criminals and seeing that they were served up for trial and punishment. He wondered how Washington knew he'd be in Santa Fe at that particular time.

"Sure a lot of ducks over there on that river," Hoyt said, pointing in the direction of the Rio Grande.

Rye did not switch his attention from the outlaw. Again his hand moved up to where the palm rested lightly on the butt of his .45.

"Heading north," he said. "That time of the year."

"A little late," the outlaw countered. "Can see some geese, too. Must've been a cold winter up north. Back where I come from—"

Abruptly the outlaw threw himself forward in the saddle. Driving his heels into the sides of his horse, he bolted for a thick stand of mesquite and other rank growth in a shallow wash, off to the side of the road.

Rye coolly drew his gun and fired. The bullet drove into Hoyt's shoulder even before he reached cover. He swayed in the saddle, began to fall. Frantically seizing the horn he caught himself, and hauling back on the reins, brought the bay to a halt. Clutching at his wounded shoulder, he twisted about and glared at the lawman now sitting quietly on the big chestnut horse he was riding as smoke curled upward from the barrel of his weapon.

"Why the hell didn't you kill me?" the outlaw demanded in a frustrated voice. "You could've done me that much of a favor."

"I'm not in the habit of doing killers like you favors," the marshal replied indifferently. "My job's to get you to El Paso, alive if possible, dead if necessary. Better stuff your bandanna into that bullet hole and stop the bleeding."

"Ain't you going to doctor me none?"

"And give you a chance to trick me so's you can make another break for it? Hell, no! It's not far now to El Paso. You can hold out till then. Move on."

Hoyt, hate glittering in his small eyes, swung the bay back onto the road and resumed the journey south, grumbling and cursing with every jolting step of his horse.

"Ain't decent to treat a man like you're doing me," he said. His left arm hung stiffly at his side, and now hooking the bay's reins over the saddle horn, he wiped at his forehead with the back of his right hand. "I'm sweating like a pig. Can't we stop over there under them trees and cool off?"

"No, keep riding," the marshal said flatly. "Just remember you brought all this on yourself. I warned you about trying to escape."

"Yeh, yeh," the outlaw said irritably. "You preach real good, but you sure don't have to treat me the way you're doing! Hell, you been hard-casing me all the way from Santa Fe."

"Only kind of treatment you deserve," Rye replied.

Rye would be glad when he got Scrub Hoyt off his hands. The outlaw was no different from the many others he'd taken in hand. Once caught, they always complained bitterly about the way they were treated. Rye had learned years ago to turn a deaf ear to their words and set his mind only to the job of staying alive while he conducted them to their destination—in this case El Paso, on the Texas–Mexico border, where he was to hand Hoyt over to the town's new marshal, Dallas Stoudenmire.

He had met Stoudenmire once before but under different conditions. A tall, dark-haired Alabaman with piercing green eyes, Dallas had earned quite a reputation as a gun fighter around the East Texas town of Columbus. Rye had arrived in the settlement a short time after a gang of outlaws had committed a robbery. The sheriff had immediately organized a posse and gone in pursuit.

"Three of them tried making a stand," Rye recalled the sheriff saying when the posse returned with four of the outlaws hanging across their saddles. "Dallas shot them down before they could pull a trigger. I got the other'n while he was sneaking off through the brush. By God, I've never seen anybody as fast with an iron as Dallas!"

That incident probably led to the officials of El Paso hiring Stoudenmire as marshal of their town, which was also a noted gathering place for outlaws on the run hoping to cross the Rio Grande and find sanctuary in Mexico when pursued by lawmen. As a result, El Paso's better elements resented the presence of such and had long sought to find a man who could and would keep the unwanted visitors on the move—or at least under control.

After a series of failures they heard of Stoudenmire and sent for him. He was still in Columbus at the time, doing nothing in particular but basking in the limelight as a fast and feared gunman. He had responded immediately to the offer made him. If any man could clean up El Paso with its problems, compounded as they were by the wild town across the border, it would be Dallas Stoudenmire, Rye reckoned.

"We got much farther to go?" Scrub Hoyt asked.

The outlaw was still holding the bandanna to his wounded shoulder. There didn't appear to be much bleeding now—a fact that meant nothing to John Rye. Outlaws got what they bargained for, he believed as cold-hearted and cruel as it might seem.

"Not far," he replied. "Maybe a mile."

The great, spreading cottonwood trees that grew along the river were no longer to be seen. The journey down from Santa Fe had been pleasant enough. He had followed the road along the east side of the Manzanos, the rugged, trailing end of the Rocky Mountains, until they had come to the canyon folks called the *Tijeras,* or the Scissors. There he had turned west through a rocky defile and continued across a broad plain until they reached the settlement of Albuquerque lying along the Rio Grande's east bank.

From there he followed the shaded stream, sometimes wide and shallow, at other times deep and treacherous, due south past an Indian village and numerous Mexican and Spanish settlements until they reached Socorro, the town at the upper end of the *Jornada del Muerto*—the Journey of the Dead—so named because of the waterless, lethal conditions it presented travelers making the trip from Mexico City north. Most pilgrims now avoided the hazardous route but there were still many unaware of the dangers who followed the ancient trail.

From Socorro on south the early summer heat had become more noticeable, and despite the broadly spreading trees that cast deep shade along the river bank, it was warm. Rye had long since discarded his wool poncho and heavy cord pants in favor of a pair of lighter weight ones, as well as changing his thick, shield front shirt to one of light cotton texture. But such was to be expected, Rye knew from experience. El Paso, lying pretty much in the center of a bowl of rocks, was always a hot place in the summer.

Small adobe huts began to appear along the roadside, each with a small garden of corn, tomatoes, and other vegetables. There were a few orchards apricots, apples, and peaches—the fruit still small and undeveloped. A pale dust pall hung over it all, stirred up by a light wind coming in from the west.

"Is this here where we're headed, or is it just another of them damn settlements?" Hoyt asked as they rode slowly toward a collection of huts and houses.

"This is it," Rye said, nodding. "Main part of

town's just around those trees. Jail will be on the right-hand side of the street. You've made it alive this far so don't push your luck by doing something foolish."

CHAPTER 2

Stoudenmire had changed little since their casual meeting two years ago, Rye thought as he made his way along the dry, dusty street to the Central Hotel, recommended by the El Paso lawman as the best place in town to put up.

He had left the chestnut in the livery stable near the jail along with the rented horse Scrub Hoyt had been riding. His thought was to return the bay to its owner in Santa Fe when he headed back in that direction. It would not be out of his way, for he intended to continue on to Wichita as planned.

It felt good inside the Central out of the day's heat. After registering at the desk where an elderly, gray-haired man wearing pince-nez glasses had greeted him solemnly. Rye crossed to a side door that led to a saloon. He'd have himself a couple of drinks, clean up, eat, lay around for the rest of that day and the night, and then head north in the morning.

The saloon had only a half a dozen patrons at that late morning hour, all of whom were seated around a table engaged in a game of poker. Passing them by, Rye took a place at the short, polished bar.

"Whiskey, your good stuff," he said as the barkeep welcomed him with a nod.

The sound of running horses in the street temporarily broke the quiet but aroused no interest among the saloon's customers or the full-mustached bartender who shoved a glass in front of the marshal and filled it from a freshly uncorked bottle.

"Just passing through?" the man behind the counter asked, swiping at the surface of the bar with a towel. "Don't recollect seeing you in here before."

"Just passing through," Rye agreed, and turning about, put his attention on the card players.

"Hell, I wasn't meaning to be nosey," the barkeep said in an aggrieved voice. "Just being friendly."

Rye tossed off his drink, smiled briefly, and pointed at the bottle of liquor and his empty glass. "Once more," he said. "And no offense taken. Been in the saddle for quite a spell."

The barman refilled Rye's glass, stepped back. Smoothing his mustache he shook his head. "Man can sure get tired of riding. Found that out when I was riding fence for a rancher north of here. Didn't know that leather could get so damn hard. Expect that's what set me to tending bar."

"Was through here a couple of years ago," Rye said. "Don't remember this place being here."

"It wasn't. Neither was I."

"Guess that makes us both sort of strangers," Rye said, and crossing to one of the tables sat down.

He hoped that by the time he got to Wichita there'd be some word from Washington on his reappointment as a special marshal. Originally the job had been conferred upon him by Rutherford Hayes, but the new president, James Garfield, had been elected and so far he had not seen fit to renew the appointment.

Whether Garfield did or not was immaterial to Rye. He liked the prestige of being a federal marshal and of working with lawmen throughout the country, but if the new president had decided to abolish the job or had someone else in mind for the badge, all well and good. He'd simply go back to bounty hunting—a semi-lawman profession that not only paid equally well or better but also afforded the same free lifestyle so favored by Rye.

A half smile parted his lips. He reckoned folks would stop calling him the Doomsday Marshal if that came to pass. He'd not miss it. The descriptive name he'd acquired because of his devotion to duty had never pleased him. He had done nothing to discourage its usage, however, as it seemed often to have an intimidating effect on outlaws and thus made his job easier.

Regardless of whether he wore a star or not, he reckoned he'd always be a lawman of some kind. It was in his blood, had been since he was a young man, and doing any other kind of work was as foreign to him as the stars were from the black lava beds that scarred the southwestern countryside.

Things wouldn't be the same, though, and not being a federal marshal would take some getting used to, Rye thought as he stared into his still-full glass of whiskey. A tall man with dark, curly hair and thick overhanging brows shading near colorless blue eyes, Rye had a long face, a full mustache, and at the moment, a bristling beard, as he'd not taken time on the trail to shave.

A cold, ruthless-looking man accustomed to dealing with the most dangerous and deadly outlaws, he had earned his spurs first as a Tennessee Confederate cavalryman, after which he became bounty hunter, deputy sheriff, gold train guard, a town marshal, shotgun rider on a stagecoach, and several short-lived positions of a similar nature.

A loner in the true sense of the word, he had no close acquaintances, and if there were any living relatives he took great care to never mention them —likely for their own good, for through the years the number of threats on his life had grown impressively.

There were many who accused John Rye of being too cold, too unfeeling in his handling of outlaws, but he brushed such complaints aside if he deigned to take notice of them at all. An outlaw killer knew what he was doing when he committed his crime and thus should expect to face the consequences.

Dressed now in a lightweight shirt and pants in deference to the border heat, stove pipe boots equipped with army spurs, blue bandanna, a flat crowned dark hat, a full cartridge belt with its holstered .45 Colt encircling his lean waist, he appeared every bit the single-minded, invulnerable lawman feared and respected throughout the frontier.

Rye stirred slightly, caution lifting within him as he became aware of a man entering the saloon and bearing directly toward him. Leaning back in his chair Rye watched the individual—tall, an aged misshapen hat tipped forward over his eyes, wearing ordinary duck pants, linsey-woolsey shirt, rundown boots, scarred leather vest, and walking with a limp—draw near. As the man came to a halt before the marshal he brushed his hat to the back of his head.

"Howdy, John—"

Rye frowned as he studied the speaker. There were two small holes on the heart side of the sun bleached vest where a lawman's star or badge had been pinned. Reaching out slowly he accepted the hand outstretched to him. In that same moment recognition came to him.

"Hugh! Hugh Ligon! Didn't recognize you!"

"Been a while, and things have changed a mite," Ligon said, sitting down in one of the chairs.

Rye motioned for the barkeeper to bring a glass and the bottle of whiskey. "Did you get yourself shot up? Notice you limping."

"Got into a shootout over on the salt flats a time back, right after I last seen you, in fact." Ligon paused as the barkeep arrived and set a glass before him. Filling the container, he placed the bottle in the center of the table and returned to his counter.

"Slug got me in the knee, left it stiff," Ligon continued. "One that hit me in the shoulder didn't do me no good, either. Made my arm kind of stiff."

"Sure sorry to hear about that. You quit the Rangers? I see you're not wearing a badge."

Ligon tossed off his drink and then shook his head. "Weren't my idea. They retired me, but I reckon I can't blame them. A crippled-up man ain't of much use to anybody."

Ligon's weathered features had tightened as he spoke. They were about the same age, Rye guessed. It was sad to think that a man of Hugh's experience had been forced to quit. He had a good record with the Rangers.

"Was talking to Stoudenmire a bit ago," Ligon said, refilling both his and the marshal's glasses. "Said you'd brung in that killer that busted out of prison a year or so ago."

Rye nodded, took up his glass and extended it toward Ligon. "*Salud!*" he murmured as the containers clinked together. "Brought him down from Santa Fe."

They downed their whiskies together, set the empty glasses back on the table. "The sheriff was figuring to do the job but he got bunged up. I happened to be in Santa Fe so the chief marshal handed me the job. What're you doing nowadays if you're not riding with the Rangers?"

"Not much of anything. Still got a place out at the edge of town—same one I had when my wife was alive. Grow about everything I eat. Help out Stoudenmire whenever he needs somebody to serve papers or be the jailer. How long are you aiming to be in town?"

"Pulling out tomorrow morning."

Ligon swore softly and glanced about. The card game was breaking up and two new customers were now standing at the bar. "Was hoping you'd be hanging around for a spell. I'm sort of needing help."

Rye frowned. "What kind?"

Hugh leaned forward, elbows on the table. "Got a friend—a Ranger—in bad trouble. Can't do nothing for him alone."

"Do I know him?"

Ligon looked away as if hoping to avoid an answer. Then: "I reckon you do. It's Will Dancy."

John Rye's square jaw hardened and a glint came into his eyes. Dancy was no friend of his—had never been, and never would be.

"I know you and Will never did hit it off so good but—"

"Little hard to forget his opinion of me."

"Expect it is," Ligon said shaking his head. "That was a failing of Will's, always shooting off his mouth and saying the wrong things at the wrong time."

"The way he feels about me, can't see as I've got any call to help him."

"I realize that, John. Know just how you feel, but he's a fellow lawman, and he's in the hands of the worst bunch of outlaws that've come along in years —some Comancheros. They're holding him prisoner down in Mexico."

"If it's a reward they're after, why—"

"Not it from what I've been able to learn. Hacho, the Comanchero chief or leader seems to be holding Will there because he's a Ranger, a lawman; showing off what a big man he is."

"What's wrong with the Rangers? Why don't they go in after him?"

"Expect they would if they could, but right now the Mexican government and ours ain't on speaking terms. They're feuding over something some politician done. The Rangers and the army have been ordered not to cross the border. I guess the Mexicans've been told the same thing by their *políticos.*"

Rye twirled his empty whiskey glass between a

thumb and forefinger and stared off through the open doorway of the saloon. "Overrated" was one of the things Dancy had said of him. "The president's pet; a little town marshal with too much authority; a man getting a lot of credit for doing what any ordinary Ranger does every day." These comments Dancy had loudly proclaimed—but never in Rye's presence.

"Have you tried getting somebody else to go in after him?" Rye asked. "I'd as soon stay out of it."

"I've hit up a half a dozen other men that could maybe pull off the job, but they all turned me down. Reckon you're my last hope."

Rye continued to look off through the open doorway. He could imagine what sort of hell Dancy was going through; he'd had a taste of it himself from the kind of outlaws he had to deal with; but such would not compare with the cruel and inhuman treatment that a bunch of Comancheros, some Indian, some Mexican, others half breeds, could mete out to a lawman—always the prime object of their hatred.

"Do you know where this Hacho's got Dancy?"

"Sure do," Ligon said, relief showing on his face as he leaned forward again. "Leastwise we know about where. It's a place down on the Culebra River, somewheres east of Chihuahua."

"That covers a lot of territory."

"Know it sounds like it but it'll be no problem. I've got a man who'll take us right to Hacho's camp. We call him Breed. Real name's Placido something. He's part Mex and part Apache. Grew up working and living with some missionaries."

"Never figured a man could bank much on a breed. You sure he can be trusted?"

"I'll bet my bottom dollar on him! He hates Hacho and his bunch. They raided the village where him and his family lived. Murdered everybody but two young girls. Carried them off when they left. Both were Breed's sisters. There ain't nothing he won't do to get back at Hacho and his bunch."

Rye was still doubtful. "Heading down into Mexico with a half-breed carrying a big hate could be mighty dangerous."

"I'll admit that, but Placido ain't the kind that'll double-cross you. He'll do what he's told, and he'll take on a chore of doing anything he figures will hurt Hacho. He's plenty smart, too. You won't need to worry none about him pulling some fool stunt that'd foul things up for you."

Rye reached for the bottle and poured another round of drinks. The saloon was now empty except for him and Hugh Ligon, but there were several men standing just outside the door to the street holding a conversation.

"Sure like for you to go talk to him," Ligon said as the lawman refilled the glasses.

"He live around here?"

Hugh Ligon nodded as he took up his drink. "Got a 'dobe shack down along the river. Let's swallow this scamper juice, then I'll take you to meet him."

CHAPTER 3

"Town sure hasn't grown much," Rye said as Ligon led the way along the edge of the bosque bordering the river. "Looks about the same as it was when I was here a couple of years ago."

"Got about five hundred people living here, I heard the mayor say, but he figures it'll be ten times that real soon now that the railroad finally got here. That'll make it the size of Juarez—Mexican town across the river."

"I remember the place. How much farther to Breed's house? I'm not much of a hand at walking."

"Half mile or so."

Rye looked ahead at the confusion of cottonwood and other trees, tall grass, weeds and rotting stumps. A flock of ducks was slanting down out of the clear, hot sky for the river below, and immediately ahead a coyote suddenly appeared, and just as quickly vanished into the brush.

"Breed do scouting for the Rangers?"

"Has now and then," Ligon replied. "Real good at it. Knows the country around here like he does his own wife. He won't be getting paid by the company for this, though, if we go. I aim to take up a collection from the men themselves to give him if he wants pay for it."

"Why wouldn't he?"

"Like I said Breed's a man with only one partner —a big hate for Hacho and his Comancheros. It's with him all the time. Chances are he'll take us to their camp without wanting any pay at all if he figures we're out to kill Hacho and his men."

Rye shrugged, brushed at the sweat on his forehead and jaw. "Way I see it, the job is to get Dancy out, not try to kill off Comancheros."

"One job goes with the other," Ligon said, and pointed to a small adobe hut a short distance ahead. "That's his place."

Set in a clearing surrounded by chaparral and twisted Mexican elder trees, Rye saw a low, square, mud-plastered structure. A rope running from one of its corners to a close by post supported freshly washed clothes; a second, shorter line attached to the opposite side of the hut, extended to one of the trees. It sagged with strips of meat and pods of red and green chile being cured in the hot sun.

Three small children played in the yard fronting the hut, and a young woman with a pleasant, impassive face paused at the chore of washing more clothing in a wooden tub, and considered their approach with large, dark eyes. She turned to the entrance to the adobe structure and said something in Spanish. Immediately a lean, dark-haired, dark-faced man of around thirty or so stepped out to greet them. Wearing white cotton pants, a faded gray army shirt, Apache moccasins, and an old campaign hat, he leaned the rifle he had taken up, apparently as a precaution, against the wall of the hut, and unsmilingly came forward.

"Howdy, Breed," Ligon said, extending his hand. "Brung along a friend to meet you."

Placido's stolid features registered no reaction as he put his attention on Rye. Shaking hands with the one-time Ranger in the brief manner of the Mexican people, he turned to Rye and offered his hand.

Rye nodded. "Pleased to meet you. Name's John Rye."

"You a Ranger?"

"No, a U.S. Marshal."

"I've been telling him about Will Dancy," Ligon said. "Think maybe he'll be willing to go in after him if you'll guide us to the Comanchero camp."

Placido's shoulders lifted and fell. "It is far, *señor.* And there will be many dangers."

"How far?" Rye pressed.

"Five, six days to the Rio Culebra. Maybe two more to Vado."

"Vado? What's that?" Ligon asked.

"It is the village that Hacho has taken for his camp."

The children, scuffling about in the dust with a mongrel dog, began to noisily shout back and forth. Placido spoke to them harshly whereupon they hushed, and followed by the listless dog, filed into the house—all of which drew no notice from his wife or woman, whichever she was.

"That's a hell of a long trip, and a hot one, too," the marshal murmured.

It was one he was not anxious to make. First and foremost he had been in the saddle and on the move for several weeks, and was looking forward to taking it easy in Wichita for a few days—a plan that had already been thwarted once. Secondly, Will Dancy was no friend of his, and a man he held in low regard. Too, it seemed to Rye that it was a job for the Rangers, headquartered at nearby Ysleta, to bail out one of their own.

The reason they had not, according to Hugh Ligon, was trouble between the American and Mexican governments, which at the moment was forbidding not only law and military personnel from crossing the border but civilians as well. Be that as it may, the lawman was finding it difficult to believe that, if the Rangers wanted to rescue Dancy badly enough, they could have slipped a small party of men over the border under cover of darkness and freed him.

"You still willing to take us to Hacho's camp?" Ligon asked. "Can't say how much there'll be for you—twenty, maybe thirty dollars, all depending on what I can get the rest of the Rangers to chip in."

"I take you," Placido said. "When we go?"

Ligon glanced at Rye. "What do you say, John? Made up your mind yet?"

Rye looked out into the tangle of growth beyond the clearing where a flock of blackbirds were restlessly settling down in a stand of tules. Maybe he was wrong, maybe he was being petty where Will Dancy was concerned.

"The marshal—he is scared?" Placido asked bluntly.

Ligon half smiled. "Not him. He's been to hell and back many, many times."

"Then why does he not wish to go?"

"Dancy is not a friend of his."

"Is Dancy not a lawman also? Does not one

lawman stand at the side of another when he is in trouble?"

"The marshal is a busy man. He just brung in a killer that the law plans to hang, and turned him over to Stoudenmire. Can't say that he—"

"No need to explain anything to him," Rye cut in. "I don't give a damn what he thinks. Point is, can he take me to where they're holding Dancy?"

"Says he can. Says he's seen Dancy there," Ligon said, and paused. "That mean you're willing to go?"

"I'll go," the lawman said, "but it'll have to be just him and me. Never been any hand to run with a posse."

Ligon's features clouded. "Me going along hardly makes it a posse."

"I don't like saying this, Hugh, but you're in no shape to go up against what we'll likely be facing."

Ligon swore, shook his head. "Yeh, reckon you're right. I sure was counting on going along, though."

"Can see that but we'll be going right into the middle of Hacho's camp—"

"It is like a small village, *señor,*" Placido said. "There are huts, a church, a blacksmith, even a—"

"Whatever," Rye cut in. "We'll have to move in fast and quiet, and get out the same way."

"Well, if this is the way you want it," Ligon said, resigned. "Can see how I'd sort of drag you back while just you and Breed can move a lot quicker. Main thing, anyway, is to get Will out of them renegades' hands. Anything you want me to do?"

"No, I'll get my grub sack filled at the general store. Got an extra canteen on the horse that Scrub Hoyt was riding."

"You taking a pack horse?"

"No, don't want to fool with one. You sure Breed savvys enough English to do what I tell him? I'm not much on the Mex lingo."

"Like I told you, he grew up with some missionaries—"

"Forgot you told me," the marshal said and nodded to Placido. "Will you be ready to move out at first light in the morning?"

Placido shrugged. "It is best we go before that, *jefe*. The *Federales*—"

"You figure we ought to cross the river while it is still dark, that it?"

"It is best. Also we must cross far below here where there is small chance of being seen."

"I'll have to leave that part up to you. Now, what about grub? You want to bring your own. Won't need to, I'll have plenty for both of us. Be bringing some grain for the horses, too."

"I will have my own. Also, there will be rabbits and birds along the river to kill."

"Suit yourself. Now, do we follow the Rio Grande all the way to Hacho's camp?"

"No, Vado is on the Culebra River. It is two days ride west from the Rio Grande."

"All open country?"

"There is much of such. We will follow the *calle oriente*—the east road along the river. Sometimes it is close, sometimes it turns away. It is like many rivers in one, for in places it is narrow and deep, a prisoner between high cliffs. Or perhaps there is only one cliff and the other side is flat and with much sand."

"How about grass for the horses?"

"At times it is of plenty, other times it is thin and dry, which is how you will find it on the desert. There are places of trees, and places where there are none. It is so all the way to where it meets the sea—the *golfo*—the gulf as it is now called. Once I was there with my father. It is a great river, like several as I have said. Once it was called the Rio Bravo, but what it is called now is better, for it is a very large river."

"I've been down in that neck of the woods, John," Ligon said, a hopeful note in his voice. "Know it pretty well, in fact. You still dead set on me not going?"

Rye nodded. "I figure it's best for all of us."

Ligon sighed heavily. "Was scared you'd say that. I owe Dancy a big favor. Was hoping to pay him back."

"I'll do it for you," Rye said, and turned to Placido. "Where do we meet, and when?"

"I come for you, *jefe*. Where do you stay?"

"I'll be at the livery stable by the hotel, ready to ride two hours before first light. Will that give us enough time to cross the river?"

"Yes, it is good," Placido replied.

CHAPTER 4

"You looking for there to be many Comancheros hanging around close to the river?" Rye asked as, side-by-side, he and Placido rode quietly along in the half dark of early morning. "I'd heard the Mexican army had pretty well cleaned them out."

Placido shrugged, his dark face shining faintly in the pale light. He was dressed as he was earlier, Rye noted, except that he now had a knife hanging at his side and a bandolero of cartridges across one shoulder. His rifle was in a boot slung from the saddle. It bore the stamped insignia of the U.S. Army as did the canteen, also tied to the hull. A flour sack of grub and a blanket were lashed to the saddle as well, being secured behind the cantle with several of the skirt's leather strings.

"The Comancheros are never gone. Some, but not all," Placido replied in a low voice. "They are here, they are there, like the wind. It is hard to know where to find them."

"I've never run up against them before," the lawman said. "Heard they were plenty mean, though."

"Such is true, *señor*. Only the dead do not fear them."

They were moving east through the dense band of brush that bordered the Rio Grande. El Paso and the Mexican city of Juarez now lay several miles behind them. Shortly, the dense growth of the bosquet began to thin and the lawman caught the glint of the river off to their right.

"Here is where we will cross," Placido said, veering the dusty brown horse he was riding into that direction. "Here there is no *arena movediza*—quicksand as you would say in your language—but there are the *Federales.*"

"They patrol the river?"

"You will see."

Keeping in the shadows of the trees and brush, they rode directly up to where the Rio Grande, little more than a dozen yards in width at that point, lay glinting dully before them in the moon and starlight. Almost at once two soldiers riding slowly, heads bent low, appeared on the opposite bank.

"They sleep," Placido commented dryly.

Rye watched the *Federales* pass along the far bank of the stream. Placido did not stir, and a few minutes later the two soldiers again appeared, this time coming from the opposite direction.

"There is a turn in the river. They ride to there, then they turn and come back. When they have gone by and can no longer be seen, that is when we must cross."

Rye nodded his understanding. "Say when you are ready—"

"It is best you follow close behind me. There is *arena movediza* in some places, but not so much as there is farther up the river."

Again Rye signified his understanding. It was only smart to heed the words of a man so thoroughly familiar with the area. The lawman was feeling much better about Placido. Some of the doubts he'd harbored earlier had faded.

They crossed a narrow strip of spongy, grass-covered ground to the river, rode down a slight incline that evidently had seen previous use. The horses slowed as they waded into the muddy water, knee deep to them immediately, and then moved on without hesitation into the belly-high main current. Placido held to a straight course until halfway across, but as they approached a circular sandbar, he swung to the left, avoiding the smooth formation.

"It is here we must use care," he said, his glance sweeping back and forth along the river's edge. "We must watch not only for the quicksand but also the soldiers."

They reached the opposite shore and rode quickly into the dense brush without incident, having avoided the treacherous, loose, underwater footing, thanks to the skill and knowledge of Placido, and seeing only a small pack of gray wolves—*lobos*, he called them—that vanished as suddenly into the shadows as they had appeared.

Heading into the rank growth Placido led the way southward along a maze of low, chaparral-covered hillocks, pressing on steadily until full daylight when he halted in a thin grove of cottonwood and other trees. There was but little brush for cover making it far from an ideal place to stop, and while there had been no sign of pursuit, John Rye was far from being at ease.

Ordinarily alone and on his own under similar circumstances, and in country with which he was not familiar, Rye could now only feel uncertain, heading into a dangerous land with a partner he scarcely knew and had yet to prove that he could be trusted—all to rescue a man he did not like. But John Rye had undertaken the task and it was not in him to ever back out of a deal once made, and call it quits.

They moved on an hour or so later, keeping within the brush growing along the river whenever possible. It was pleasant riding along in the clear, early coolness. Birds were plentiful—quail, larks, a fierce-looking little sparrow hawk with a grasshopper in its hooked beak, a roadrunner that crossed their path all the while glaring balefully at them from large yellow eyes; and once a coyote, thick tail hanging low, darted across a clearing where he had been feasting on a rabbit or some other small prey, and disappeared into the brush.

As they pressed steadily on neither man broke the silence. Soon the lawman realized they were drawing closer to the desert. Gaunt cholla cactus became more plentiful as did large clumps of prickly pear and stands of catclaw. Here and there he saw giant yucca plants bristling with thick, needle-pointed stems that butcher-birds made use of as storage hooks for their food.

It began to grow warmer. Rye removed his poncho and stuffed it into the blanket roll tied to the skirt of his saddle. Placido, wearing nothing more than a light cotton shirt, pants, and moccasins, gave no notice to the rising temperature other than to brush at the damp shine on his dark face occasionally.

Near noon, with a ragged line of low lying hills

jutting off to the west Placido slowed the pace. The horses were showing wear from the heat and the constant fast pace. Cutting left toward the river, still close by, he continued for a short distance and drew to a halt. Dismounting, they rested the chestnut and the brown for several minutes until they had cooled down, and then led them down to the water where they satisfied their thirst. That accomplished, Placido then continued on a hundred yards or so to a small clearing where the horses could graze while they rested.

"Good time for us to eat, too," Rye said, digging into his grub sack for one of the bread and meat sandwiches he'd prepared at the hotel's restaurant.

Placido nodded agreement and began to search around in the flour sack containing his stock of grub, producing finally a corn tortilla in which meat and chile had been wrapped.

The heavy silence between them continued as they sat in the comparative coolness along the river, each man deep in his own thoughts. After a time Placido finished his meal and moved off in the direction of the river, apparently for a drink. Rye, also through with the noonday lunch, contented himself with a swallow from one of his canteens. As he was corking the metal container Placido returned, his dark features set in grim lines.

"*Federales*—they come," he said, and hurried off toward the horses.

Rye swore softly. They had congratulated themselves too soon. "Where are they?" he asked, catching up.

"Along the river. They come this way," Placido

said as they reached the horses. "I see them when I drink."

"How many?" the lawman asked, gathering up the chestnut's reins.

"Five, maybe six. They are close."

"It's best we don't make a run for it then," Rye said, and leading the gelding, crossed to the edge of the clearing. Stopping there, he turned to Placido. "You figure they'll come by here?"

"It is likely, *jefe.*"

"Then we'll stay put, let them do the moving about," the lawman said, and moved on into the brush and high weeds.

Shortening his grasp on the chestnut's reins, he pulled the horse's head sharply about, as he had done many times before, and pushing hard against the animal's body, forced him to fall, immediately placing a knee on the horse's neck and pressing on the head to keep it prone. Glancing around he saw that Placido had followed his example with the brown he was riding.

Within only minutes the *Federales*—members of the Mexican cavalry—appeared. They were apparently following the river back to Juarez, probably returning from a mission or an excursion of some sort into the country. Clad in the bright blue and red uniforms currently in use at the time, they looked worn and dusty, and when they drew abreast no more than ten yards distant Rye could see that their horses were well used.

The *Federales* halted. In the suddenly tense hush, John Rye removed his hand from the chestnut's neck and drew his sixgun. Placido, face wooden, quietly pulled his rifle from the saddle boot, and laid it on the leaf littered ground beside him. Insects, disturbed by the soldiers, had ceased their noisy clacking and the tight hush that claimed the clearing and nearby brush was momentarily absolute.

"*Ai—eee,*" one of the men sighed loudly as he dismounted. Pushing his officer's shako to the back of his head, he walked stiffly over to a small backwater at the river's edge, and squatting, dipped water with a cupped hand to his mouth. Shortly the remaining men, ground-reining their horses, joined him.

Abruptly Placido's horse stirred and struggled to rise, the sound overloud in the hush. Instantly Placido threw himself upon the animal's neck and head, pressing the horse back to the grassy ground. Rye tensed, readied his gun. One of the soldiers paused, turned his attention toward the high weeds. The man beside him hesitated also and glanced in the direction of the lawman and Placido. In the dappled shade the sun blackened skin of the *Federales* glowed with sweat. Rye and his partner remained motionless, scarcely breathing as they rode out the tense moments. And then the first of the two soldiers shrugged as he loosened his collar.

"*Un animal,*" he said and continued on to where his companions squatted at the edge of the backwater.

The *Federale* with him also shrugged and followed, removing his ornate headgear as he did.

Tension eased in John Rye. He glanced at Placido and grinned. The half-breed nodded slightly. The tight moments had passed but neither man released the weapon held ready in his hand.

In the warm quiet the soldier's horses abandoned for the time, and smelling the water, began to drift toward the river. Insects resumed their cacophony and high overhead a large hawk, or perhaps it was a young golden eagle, soared effortlessly about on the hot air currents rising from the desert.

For several minutes the soldiers remained by the river talking and laughing while they smoked numerous slim brown paper cigarettes and the horses slaked their thirst nearby; and then the officer gave the word and the others, gathering up the reins of their mounts, followed him back into the clearing.

The insects once more fell silent and a pair of doves nesting in a nearby cottonwood tree fluttered noisily off toward the desert, the sound of their beating wings drawing a laugh from some of the soldiers startled by the unexpected sound.

The *Federales* did not go into the saddle, but holding to their lines, led the horses across the clearing and on up the trail along the river, staying well in the shade as they did. Evidently they had been in the saddle for a considerable length of time and were relieving their aching muscles by continuing their journey on foot for awhile.

When the sounds of their passage could no longer be heard Rye gave the signal, and getting to his feet, allowed the chestnut to rise.

Nodding to Placido, also up with his horse again on all four feet, he said, "Let's move out of here. Got nothing against the Mexican army so I don't want any shootout with any of them."

CHAPTER 5

They continued on a southerly direction for the following three days, keeping to the cooler area along the river when it was possible to do so. The desert to the west of them became more and more evident with giant cactus and yucca plants, tall, eerie-looking growths that Placido called *agaves*, to be seen everywhere. The heat had increased as had the presence of scorpions, spiny lizards, and large, hand-sized tarantulas—all of which drew little attention from Placido.

On the afternoon of the fourth day as they were resting in the coolness of a small grove near the river, Placido said, "We have moved very fast, *jefe*. In the morning we will come to the Culebra."

Rye, smoking one of his few remaining stogies, nodded. "The Culebra—that's the name of the other river you mentioned—"

"It is, *señor*. It turns away from the Rio Grande and runs to the southwest."

"All the way to the Sierra Madre?"

"That I cannot say for I have never been that far to the southwest. It is a small river and there is not always water of sufficiency. Nor is there always brush and trees to furnish hiding. There will be danger of being seen by Hacho's men."

"Means we best do our traveling at night."

"It is best."

Off in the distance a coyote barked into the closing day. Rye listened briefly and then flicking the ashes off his cigar said, "You have much truck with these Comancheros?"

Placido frowned. "I do not understand your meaning—"

"Have you been around them much? Have you done any dealing with them?"

"No man deals with the Comancheros—only the Comanches and those merchants who purchase women and men from them," Placido replied, his features darkening. "To deal, as you say, with the Comancheros is to deal with death."

"Always heard they were the worst kind of outlaws. Put their time in robbing and killing pilgrims and ranchers."

"Such is true—to rob and kill, that is their life. Also it is to make captives of those they believe will bring to them profit."

"Slaves?"

"*Sí.* The young women they will sell to the *casas de las putas*—the houses of the whores—as you would say in your tongue. The young men and boys they sell to the gold and silver mines."

"What about the older people?"

"For them there is death, sometimes at once, other times they are tortured and made sport of."

Rye stirred, looked off toward the low mountains in Texas on the far side of the river. He could imagine what Will Dancy, being a Ranger, was going through. Hacho and his blood-thirsty followers would be making life a hell for him.

"You know if they're holding any other prisoners besides Dancy?"

Placido's shoulders moved slightly in an indication of uncertainty. "I do not know, *jefe*, but it would be strange if there are not. Many wagons pass this way going to Chihuahua, or are nearby on the other side of the Rio Grande. Also there are ranches and *haciendas*—farms you would say—in many places on both sides of the river. It is not only food Hacho takes from them but all else that he wants."

Rye turned his attention back to Placido, and then to the open desert beyond him. "If the country's so overrun by Comancheros I can't figure why we haven't spotted a bunch of them by now. All we've seen are those soldiers."

"Perhaps that is why—there are *Federales* around. But as I have said the Comancheros are like the wind. They are here, they are there, but you do not see them—often when it is too late."

"That what happened to your family? Ligon said—"

"I do not like to remember—yet I never forget," Placido said, rolling another of his slim, brown paper cigarettes. "I do not let myself forget."

"I think he said you saw it all—"

Placido nodded. Finishing his cigarette, he placed it between his thin lips, lit it with a match and blew a small cloud of smoke into the hot, motionless air. "I was on the hill that stands behind our village. The house of my parents is below, near the foot. It was near the noon of the day and all was quiet. I was resting from searching for a strayed calf. There was nothing, no horse or man to be seen anywhere. Of a sudden there were gunshots and much yelling. I ran to where I could see better. Many riders—Comancheros—were in the yard of my parent's home.

"I saw them shoot my father and then my mother while they enter the house. They return with my two sisters and other belongings that was their desire. I shout at them and start down the hill to stop them."

"You have a gun?"

"No, I have only my knife. They only laugh at me. Then I see the leader raise his rifle to fire at me. I do not know what occurred after that. The bullet strike the side of my head and I am unconscious. I knew later that the leader was Hacho."

"What about your sisters?"

"I never see them again."

"They take any other women?"

"My sisters were but young girls, *jefe*. One was twelve years of age, the other fifteen. They were not women. There were but three other families in the village. All were of the age of my parents. Hacho and his *asesinos* killed them also."

"Didn't the army do something about it?"

"I travel to the nearest *presidio* where there are soldiers. They send a number of men but of course they are much too late. They search around for a while and then leave. They can find no Comancheros."

Rye swore quietly. "I can see why you hate them so—"

"All Mexicans hate them," Placido said. "There are those who—"

Placido paused, raised his hand for silence. In the

late afternoon light his strong features appeared bronze, silhouetted against the harsh glow.

"Someone comes," he murmured, and tossing aside the cigarette, took up his rifle and got to his feet.

Rye was upright instantly, .45 also in hand. He could hear approaching horses in that next moment. They were coming down river following the line of brush and other growth that bordered the stream.

"Comancheros," Placido murmured. Crouched low he had moved to the fringe of the thick growth where he had a better view of the trail. "They have a prisoner."

Keeping well in the brush the lawman also crossed to a point that afforded him a clearer look at the trail. He had spoken too soon, he thought wryly. Just when he had concluded there were no Comancheros in the area they appeared.

"How many?" he asked, edging up closer to Placido.

"Four—and the captive."

Rye saw the party at that moment. The outlaws were wearing broad Mexican hats, assorted items of clothing, and crossed bandoleros, the loops of which were filled with brass cartridges that glinted in the sunlight. The prisoner, hands tied behind his back, head down, rode slumped in the saddle.

Rye turned to Placido. The half-breed, hunched even lower than before, was making his way to a thick stand of brush along the trail near where the Comanchero party would pass. Placido's face was set, expressionless, but there was a hardness to it that bespoke the hatred he felt.

Taking his cue from Placido the marshal also edged up to where he would be closer to the trail. He wasn't able to tell anything about the Comancheros' prisoner as yet, but the fact that he was a captive warranted rescuing. No one, regardless of identity, should be left to the mercy of Hacho and his renegades.

"They come," Placido warned quietly.

Rye, sixgun cocked and ready in his hand, tensed. Over to his left a snake, unaware of his presence, slithered off into the leaves and other debris, sunlight glistening on its back.

Abruptly the riders were in front of them. Rye had a glimpse of Placido, knife in his upraised hand, a chilling, nerve-shattering yell coming from his throat, launching himself at the outlaw nearest him.

The Comancheros, caught off guard, pulled to a quick stop. Confused they began to wheel their horses. Rye knocked the one in the lead, a squat, swarthy man in a red shirt, from his saddle with a bullet in his chest. Placido, astride the renegade he had attacked, and repeatedly driving the knife into the outlaw's body, continued to yell as momentum carried them both off the horse and to the ground.

Through the turmoil of milling horses, powder smoke, and dust, Rye saw one of the Comancheros whip his rifle about and snap a shot at Placido. His bullet missed, but Rye, on one knee to steady himself, did not. The outlaw threw up his hands and tumbled from the saddle.

Placido, now on his feet, lunged at the fourth man. The outlaw, hat displaced and hanging on his back from its chin string, drove spurs into his horse, whirled and ducked into the nearby brush. Instantly Rye plunged into the heavy growth after the renegade.

"Stop him!" he yelled. "He'll tell Hacho we're here!"

He caught a glimpse of the outlaw in the next moment. The man was crouched low over his horse riding recklessly at top speed through the trees and brush. The marshal fired instantly, knew as quickly that he had missed. The Comanchero, swerving in and out of the trees and brush, was an impossible target. Cursing, Rye replaced the spent cartridges in his .45 and retraced his steps to where he'd left Placido and the Comanchero prisoner.

Reaching the place where the ambush had taken place, the lawman paused. Placido was kneeling over one of the dead outlaws going through his pockets for valuables, which he transferred to his own. The captive, standing on the opposite side of the horse he was riding, hands now free, stepped into full view. Rye swore deeply. It was Hugh Ligon.

"What the hell—" he began, anger lifting within him.

"Ain't no use cussing at me, John," the ex-Ranger said. "I just had to come."

"I figured you'd stand by your word."

"I reckon I ought to've, but I got to thinking about it. Owe Will Dancy a'plenty, like I said, and letting you and Breed do my paying back just wasn't right. A man has to pay his own dues same as he has to skin his own snakes. So I up and followed you."

"And got yourself caught first off—"

"Yeh, they must've spotted me not long after I crossed the Rio and ambushed me—same as you did them."

Rye walked slowly into the small clearing. "That one getting away—that'll mean trouble if he's one of Hacho's outfit."

"Expect he is, all right. This here's Hacho's territory, and I ain't heard of no other bunch being around. That right, Breed? You think this was part of Hacho's gang?"

Placido, finished with rifling the corpses, and now wearing a second bandolero of ammunition, nodded. "It is so. All are with Hacho. There are no others."

"Sure hate letting that one get away," Rye said. "Couldn't hit him because of the brush. Expect he'll head right straight for Hacho, and tell him all about us."

"It is so, *jefe,* " Placido agreed. "We must ride fast now to the Culebra. By doing so we can perhaps fool them."

Ligon, recovering his weapons from the dead outlaw who had taken them, crossed to his horse.

"How far are we from the Culebra?" he asked. "Can we make it there by dark?"

"No, *señor,* " Placido replied. "If we are with luck we will reach it by daylight."

CHAPTER 6

Placido's prediction was right. They reached the junction where the Rio Culebra broke away from its parent, the Rio Grande, and began a meandering, twisting journey westward. The stream was low and the growth along its banks sparse and sun-punished, but it would afford fair cover, Rye figured. They halted and had a light breakfast of coffee, bacon and corn cakes fried in grease.

"We laying over here till dark?" Ligon asked.

All three men were hunched around the low fire for despite the nearby desert it was cold and the heat felt good.

Placido put his attention on Rye. "It is for you to say, *jefe.*"

"Sort of hate to waste a day just laying around here when Lord only knows what them devils are putting Dancy through," Ligon continued. "What do you think, John?"

The marshal gave the question several moments' consideration. He could understand Ligon's desire to find Will Dancy and free him from his captivity as soon as possible, but it would be foolish to jeopardize the mission by faulty judgment and being too anxious—and it was apparent that there were Comancheros in the immediate area.

"What's it like between here and this place where Hacho has his camp?" he asked.

"A flat country, but with arroyos and bluffs. There is brush and small trees along the river, in places," Placido said.

"What about the land itself? There much growing on it?"

"No, this is desert. You will find only saltbush and ocotillo, much yucca and cactus. Also there will be large clumps of creosote bush."

"Rocks?"

"There are some in places."

"There's a big sand dune out there somewhere, too," Ligon added. "Never been there but I've heard about it. They say when the wind starts blowing hard a man had best find the hindside of a hill and cover up his head and that of his horse unless he wants to get blinded. The sand, they say, is sharp as glass."

"The walking land, as some people call it, is much farther to the west," Placido said. "It is doubtful that we will have trouble from it this time of year."

"Do you think we can follow the Culebra and get to Hacho's place without being seen?"

The breed shrugged, tossed a handful of dry sticks onto the dwindling fire. "Comancheros will be plentiful now, and they will ride close to the river where it will be cooler. If we are sharp with our eyes, perhaps we will see them first."

"Can figure he'll be expecting us," Rye said. "That one that got away will put them all on guard."

"Maybe not," Ligon said. "We were headed

down the Rio Grande when you jumped that bunch. Could be Hacho will figure you were headed down the Rio, and will keep right on doing it."

Such was a possibility, the lawman realized. He glanced at Placido for approval or disagreement. He shook his head.

"Hacho has many men. He will send to watch along the Rio Grande, and others to wait along the Culebra."

That made sense to Rye. No matter which way they turned now they could expect to encounter Comancheros. "I'd like your advice," he said to Placido. "You think we ought to stay here until dark, or ride on?"

"It is for you to say, but was I the *jefe*, I would rest the horses for a time, then continue. It is known we are in the country, and the danger of encountering the Comancheros is as great here as it will be along the Culebra."

"Then we move on," Rye said, ending the discussion.

He looked off into the desert beyond the fringe of green. It was beautiful in the early morning before the blistering sun sapped the moisture from the flowers, the low-growing shrubs, and stunted trees. Only the cactus remained strong and defiant during the midday heat, having stored up its reservoir of water during the times when such was available.

They moved on after resting the animals for a little over an hour, staying close to the Culebra, brush bordered in that particular area. It was a much smaller stream than the Rio Grande, and the country lying to either side of it varied but little as they pressed steadily west for a time and then began to bend more to the south. As the day wore on the heat mounted. The scent brush along the Culebra became dry and brittle with curled leaves seeking to escape the driving rays of the sun.

The gentle beauty of the early morning altered, and it became a burning land of browned, lifeless grass, withered weeds, cowering saltbush, cactus and scarlet-crowned ocotillo plants. Several times they crossed and recrossed the Culebra, never deep at any point—a fact for which they should all be grateful, according to Placido. At times when one of the rare rainstorms struck it could become high and wild and was known to sweep a horse off its feet.

On the second day out as they plodded steadily on suffering from the heat, soaked to the skin with sweat, they spotted a party of riders off to their right, and immediately took cover in the scant growth along the stream.

"They are Comancheros," Placido said after studying them for a time. "They come from the direction of the Rio Grande, and they are of Hacho's camp since they ride for his camp."

Rye, also studying the dozen or so horsemen through the telescope he carried, shook his head. "Can't tell if they've got any captives or not."

"I do not think so, *jefe*," Placido said. "They carry much goods—much material things. It is clear they have made a raid and did not trouble to take prisoners."

"Probably hit some poor pilgrim moving west and didn't figure the folks in the wagons was worth fooling with," Hugh Ligon said.

"Also it could have been a *rancho* or a *hacienda* they have struck," Placido murmured.

The Comancheros were all well armed, the marshal noted, each carrying a rifle, side arm and a knife along with crossed bandoleros of ammunition. It would be no easy task to rescue Will Dancy from such men—that was becoming more apparent as they drew nearer to the outlaw stronghold. They were all well equipped and mounted, to which should be added the fact the Comancheros would be of a considerable number. The lawman gave that thought that night as they camped in a brushy hollow a short distance from the river.

"How many men do you figure Hacho's got?" he asked Placido when the meal of cold meat, dry bread and water was over.

"It is not easy to say," Placido replied. "They come and they go, and many are killed by the *Federales*."

"Make a guess."

"I would say there are always a half-hundred with him, but perhaps more, perhaps less."

The answer wasn't a great deal of help, but it did afford Rye with some idea of what they would be going up against.

"You got any idea how we can get Will away from them?" Ligon asked, also directing his question to Placido.

"No, *señor*, that I cannot say. It will be very hard. There are always many Comancheros in camp. Others will be away but the camp is never forsaken. Also there are the women."

"Does Hacho usually go on those raids?" Rye wondered, swiping at the sweat still beading his forehead. The sun had gone but the intense heat still prevailed.

"Many times he does not. He has a great longing for the women and spends much time with them. It is said that he has ten, perhaps twelve wives."

"Are they ones he's taken captive?"

"Sometimes, but the women with greater beauty —the ones with light hair and eyes—he saves to sell. If they are untouched they will bring much more money than those who have been married."

Rye swore harshly. Men who dealt in women always filled him with rage. Such was doubly true where the Comancheros and their helpless victims were concerned.

"When do we get to this Vado?" he asked, finishing off the last of the bread and meat sandwich he was eating. He'd be glad when they got to a place where they could risk a hot meal complete with coffee.

"Tomorrow, *jefe*. By the hour of mid-afternoon."

"Good. Like to get a look at the camp in daylight."

"That will be possible, *jefe*. And it also possible you will see Hacho."

"That'll suit me fine."

"It is hoped such a meeting will go well for you. I myself will pray to the Blessed Virgin to protect you."

"Better ask her to look after all three of us," Hugh Ligon said, and then smiling quizzically at Placido, added, "After what happened to your family you still believe in getting help from this here Blessed Virgin you're talking about?"

Placido shrugged. "It is good to have faith in

something, *señor*," he said, and rising walked off to where the horses were tethered.

Ligon's eyes were on the half-breed for a long minute and then hawking, he spat into the fire. "Personally I'm put my faith in this," he said, patting the gun strapped to his side. "Ain't never failed me when I needed it. How about you, John?"

Rye smiled faintly. "I welcome all the help I can get," he said, and coming to his feet, moved off through the increasing darkness toward the river.

Placido's estimation of time required to reach Hacho's camp was accurate. After following the stream for most of that next day, seeing several parties of riders come and go, Placido halted in a narrow wash not far from the Culebra.

"We are now close," he said. "It is necessary we use much care."

"Where's the camp?" Ligon asked, checking the loads in his sixgun.

Placido pointed to a low rise east of them. "It is beyond that, in a deep place by the river. We will cross to the little hill but it must be done quickly. To be seen by someone will bring many of Hacho's men."

Waiting until they could see no riders or anyone on foot in any direction, they crouched low on their horses and broke from the brush and rode hard for the arroyo at the foot of the rise. They made it without being seen—insofar as they knew —in fast time. Pulling to a stop Placido gestured with a thumb at the hill's crest.

"From there it is possible to look down upon the camp of the Comancheros."

Rye studied it briefly. "There any tall brush up there?"

"Only bushes, *jefe*. It will be best if we leave the horses here in these paloverde trees. They perhaps will not be seen if someone comes down the river, as did we."

Rye nodded, and with Ligon and the half-breed, dismounted and started up the steep, brushy slope. Reaching the summit, they dropped flat onto the still hot sandy ground and worked their way to the opposite side of the rise. Reaching there they drew to a halt, unwilling to chance going any further along the slight decline that was now before them.

"Looks like a town—a small village," Ligon said.

"It was so once, *señor*, " Placido murmured.

Rye considered the few scattered adobe huts: a weathered, sun-bleached church and a single large building that may have once been a general mercantile store. Once families lived there, growing their gardens, raising their sheep or cattle, visiting their church, and enjoying a peaceful life. And then the Comancheros had come and taken over.

"There's Will," Ligon said in a quick, taut way.

The lawman followed the one time Ranger's leveled finger. Dancy lay sprawled in the driving sunlight in front of the larger building, evidently a sort of headquarters. A chain was fastened to a belt that encircled his waist. The opposite end of the string of shining steel links was attached to a thick post erected where it was in full view of not only the building's entrance but most of the huts as well.

CHAPTER 7

Ligon swore deeply. "What've they done to him?" he muttered. "Them damn savages, they—"

"He's alive," Rye said. "Reckon you could say that's what counts."

"It is a pleasure of Hacho—a sport as I have said. He many times chains a prisoner, one he believes is of no value, to the post so that much sport can be made of him. I have heard of women, without clothes, receiving the same treatment when they are of no use to him."

Ligon swore again. "We've got to get Will out of there, John—"

"We will," the marshal said grimly, but accomplishing the fact could be difficult, he knew.

Eyes narrowed to cut down the glare, Rye studied the Comanchero camp. The larger house, of adobe and wood, was in the center of what had once been the small village. A wide porch extended across its width, and the door which opened to the inside of the structure was about halfway along its length. He could see high, small windows in the side wall visible to him.

Not far from where the Ranger lay in the sweltering sun, was a water well and horse trough. A pump, provided at considerable labor and expense by the previous inhabitants of the village, replaced the original windlass and bucket arrangement, all of which was just outside the reach of Will Dancy.

Scattered about on the barren, hard-packed ground both in front and on two sides of the main structure were adobe huts of various sizes, and all in varying stages of neglect. It was evident that Hacho's men and their women put in little time maintaining their quarters—probably because they knew only too well that they could be called upon to abandon the settlement at any time, and on short notice, should a strong force of soldiers mount an attack.

Behind the main building Rye could see several corrals, some of which contained horses, while others held mules and cattle. Nearby was another adobe building, one somewhat larger than the huts. A rusting old forge standing in its entrance indicated that it once housed a blacksmith shop. Farther on were the skeletal remains of several wagons. The canvas had been stripped from the bows and the wood of their beds pirated and likely used as fuel, all no doubt having been taken in raids. The fate of their owners could be only a matter of grim speculation.

Two men came from the main house, sunlight glinting off the silver decorations of their wide *sombreros* and concho embellished clothing. They swaggered to the pump and horse trough. Dancy had moved about and was seeking relief from the burning sun in the slim shadow of the post to which he was chained. The Comancheros halted at the trough, and taking up the tin dipper hanging from the pump, levered it full of cool water, and in turn satisfied their thirsts.

Dancy stirred, sat up and looked hopefully toward the pair. Rye could see the Ranger's lips move, guessed he was asking for water. The second outlaw continued to drink, refilled the dipper, and pulling off his hat, poured the contents of the tin container over his head. As the water cascaded down his face and neck onto his lace fronted shirt both men laughed, and replacing the dipper, returned to the house.

"He is a man with much luck," Placido said. "They have left him with his clothing."

Ligon nodded. "Got his boots, pants and shirt, all right. Expect that's his hat over there on top of that other post—out of his reach."

Off in one of the huts there was some sort of commotion. A woman cried out as if hurt, and then shortly a man appeared, and walking stiffly and angrily, headed for the main house.

"I reckon there was an argument between him and his woman," Ligon said. "Now he's going in and shoot the bull with the rest of the bunch."

"And also to drink tequila," Placido added. "Soon he will be very drunk."

Rye, finished with familiarizing himself with the layout of the camp, pulled back into the chaparral, and idly watched the outlaw cross to the structure and enter.

"Expect most of Hacho's bunch are in there taking it easy—*siesta* I think you call it."

Placido nodded. "It is the time of day when such is done. But I do not think all of the Comancheros are in there, or in the huts with their women. There will be others in the hills and along the river taking rest while they watch for travelers."

"Or getting ready to raid some ranch or farm," Ligon said. "You thinking up an idea, John—like going down there after Will right now?"

"Not yet."

Ligon swore, mopped at the sweat on his face. "Hell, we just can't set around! That man's dying an inch at a time."

"I realize that," Rye said, "but we'd be fools not to get this all figured out ahead of time. One thing, we'll need another horse."

"It will be only in darkness that he can be set free," Placido said. He was stretched out full length in the brush, hat tipped down over his eyes to shade them from the sun.

"Only chance we'll have," the lawman agreed. "We'll wait till night and things are quiet, slip down there, cut that belt the chain's fastened to, and then make a run for the horses."

"Can take one of their's for Will. Plenty of them in that end corral," Ligon said. "Ought to have ours waiting somewhere close by, too."

"We'll picket them by that corral—" Rye began, and paused.

One of the Comanchero women had emerged from a hut on the far side of the hardpack. White shirt unbuttoned in deference to the heat, full skirt brushing the dusty, littered ground as she walked, and barefooted, she crossed to the pump, and, paying no attention at all to the prisoner nearby, had a drink. Then, dark hair glinting in the sunlight, and thirst satisfied, she leisurely made her way to the main house.

"Dancy will need a weapon."

"I'll give him my rifle," Ligon said at once. "Can

make do myself with my six-shooter. Who do you figure on cutting Will loose?"

"You and me—one to see to him, the other to stand watch. We'll leave it up to Breed to move the horses and have one ready for Dancy."

Rye glanced at Placido to see if he'd heard and understood. The half-breed was snoring faintly, oblivious as well as uncaring insofar as the danger that lay before him was concerned.

"Expect the best time to make our move will be in the early morning, after we're sure everybody's bedded down."

Ligon nodded. "Let's just keep hoping they all do that, and don't stay up all night hell-raising and drinking."

"We'll have to figure on that," the marshal said, staring off across the desert, which was shimmering with the afternoon's heat. "One thing bothers me— that man that got away from us back up the river, he's bound to have ridden here and told Hacho about us."

"Ain't no doubt of it—"

"Then why didn't we run into some of the Co-mancheros standing guard and waiting for us when we came in? And there don't seem to be anybody on watch around the camp. I figured Hacho'd have a welcoming committee waiting for us somewhere along the Culebra River, and for sure around the camp."

"Sure is a puzzlement, all right," Ligon agreed.

"Only thing that makes sense is what we thought earlier—that Hacho believes we were on our way down the Rio Grande and kept on going."

"Most likely," Ligon said, and reaching out,

shook Placido awake. As the man sat up he repeated the discussion that had taken place between him and Rye.

Placido shrugged. "Who can say what Hacho would do? As the *jefe* has said, it is strange we saw no Comancheros along the river, and more strange that none guard the camp. I fear there is a trick."

"What kind of a trick?" Rye asked. "We can see the whole camp from this hill. If he had men hiding around the huts we would have spotted them."

Again Placido's shoulders stirred. "I cannot say. I know only that Hacho is one that it is not safe to —how do you say—take for granted, to believe that he is unaware of our presence. He is quiet like a rattlesnake, only he gives no warning before he strikes."

"You think he knows we're here after Will?" Ligon asked.

"If he knows we are on this hill looking down upon the camp, it is a certainty. If he believes we continued down the Rio Grande he will then think it is not our purpose."

The heat in the chaparral and other ragged growth on the crest of the rise was almost unbearable. All three men were soaked with sweat and both Rye and Ligon continually brushed at the moisture coating their faces and misting their eyes. Placido, while his dark features glistened with perspiration, seemed untroubled by the discomfort. Around them insects buzzed and clacked noisily in the weeds and brush, but elsewhere and in the hot sky above there were no signs of life.

"I expect he knows we're up here," Ligon said. "Like Breed says, you can't put much past him."

"That I cannot say," Placido said. "Perhaps he does not. Perhaps he waits for men that he surely sent to search along the Rio Grande for us. When they return and report they saw nothing of us, then it is possible he will believe we are here."

"Nothing we can do about that but keep our eyes peeled," Rye said, and added, "Not a hell of a lot of sense in our setting up here roasting, either. Let's go down where the horses are. May be a bit cooler around those trees."

"For a fact," Ligon said, beginning to pull back in the chaparral. Hindered by his stiff leg and arm, he moved slowly and with effort as he retreated from the crest of the hill.

Rye was thinking that it would be a good idea to be near the horses in the event their presence was discovered by the Comancheros. They could then mount up quickly and make a run for the brush along the Culebra, where it would be easier to defend themselves.

"You want to stall around here until we go after Will?" Ligon asked, breathless and swabbing at his face and neck when they finally reached the group of paloverde trees. "Or maybe we could cut wide and get in closer to them corrals.

"We'll wait for dark before we do anything," Rye answered, and lay back in the thin shade of the paloverdes.

CHAPTER 8

A burst of gunshots awakened John Rye. Trail-wise at such moments, and schooled in a violent world where caution was a necessity for life, he lay perfectly still listening, and viewing as much of his surroundings as possible through slitted eyes. It was late in the day, and the sun was not far from setting behind the Sierra Madre on to the west. The heat had lessened but had not yet broken, a time that was still hours away.

Another blast of shots sounded. The lawman realized they were coming from the Comanchero camp on the yonder side of the rise. He sat up immediately. Something was happening in Hacho's outlaw stronghold.

"You hear all that shooting?"

At Hugh Ligon's words Rye jerked a thumb in the direction of the outlaw camp. "Coming from over there," he said, glancing about. "Where's Breed?"

Almost at once he saw movement on the crest of the hill. It was Placido. Crouched low, he was beckoning to Rye and Ligon, wanting them to join him on the top of the rise. Immediately Rye, followed by the ex-Ranger, started up the brushy slope.

"Is it the *Federales?*" the marshal asked as he gained the summit. Keeping low he moved to

Placido's side and to where he could look down on the camp.

"No, *jefe*, there has been a raid," Placido said. "Hacho and his *asesinos* have returned. They celebrate for they have brought much goods."

"Any captives?" Rye asked, putting his attention on the confusion of men, women and horses milling about on the hardpack near the base of the hill. Dust was thick and it was difficult to see what was taking place on the long porch of the main house, across the yard.

"I see none."

Ligon swore softly. "Good. The poor devils— whatever happened to them they're still better off, I reckon."

"The red-shirted one, the one with the tall hat that has much silver on it, that is Hacho," Placido murmured.

Rye fixed his eyes on the Comanchero chief as he walked over to the pump for a drink of water. Tall, dressed in gray pants embellished by conchos, a white shirt with full sleeves, a large, decorated hat hanging down his back from a short chin cord, he appeared to be a fairly young man. His boots looked to be new and the spurs strapped to them had a shine as if they, too, might be of silver. The outlaw carried two pistols and wore crossed bandoleros of ammunition, cartridges no doubt for both the handguns and the rifle that would be hanging from his saddle.

"A *brujo*," Placido said in a savage tone. "He is one possessed with the heart of the devil."

"Ain't never heard of one any worse," Ligon

agreed. "Man that kills him will sure earn a lot of extra stars in his crown."

Placido shrugged. "Like the devil, he is not easy to kill, *señor*. Many have tried, all have failed. Your friend down there—he is one that tried."

"Will tried to kill him? Hell, I didn't know he'd gone out purpose like to get Hacho. I thought he'd been caught and taken captive like a lot of others."

"He came to the camp alone, only at that time it was another village farther to the south. It was his hope, I think, to wait and find Hacho alone, but to hope for such is useless. Hacho is a man who never lets himself be alone. Thus your friend was captured by some of those who are with him."

"I'd sure like to draw a bead on him," Ligon said angrily. "A couple of .44 slugs in his head would sure do the world a lot of good—and I could do it right from here."

"Back off, Hugh," Rye said quickly, not too sure of Ligon's momentary state of mind. "Nothing would suit me more, but it'd be the wrong move to make. We'd have Comancheros swarming all over us and before we could count ten we'd be down there with Dancy, chained up to that post, too."

"Sure, you're right, John. Was only talking about my druthers—and it's Will we come to get."

"Right," the marshal said, eyes again on the commotion below. "I've got a feeling we'll have our chance to nail him again before this sashay is over with."

Hacho, thirst slaked, had moved away from the pump. At once three young women came out of the crowd and joined him, two of them attaching themselves to his arms, leaving the third to seize the

slack in a shirt sleeve and awkwardly follow along
as he headed back for the porch where the booty
taken in the raid was being pawed over by women,
men, and a few small children.

As the Comanchero leader passed by Will Dancy
he hesitated. Turning his dark face toward the
Ranger he hawked, and spat. Dancy recoiled as the
spittle struck somewhere on his body. The women
with Hacho laughed, and the one clinging to his
right arm kicked at a pile of accumulated debris
close by, showering the Ranger with dirt and other
trash. All, including several bystanders noting the
incident, laughed. Hacho said something to Dancy,
and then he and the three women continued on
toward the house.

Rye swore deeply. Hugh Ligon stirred angrily
and muttered irritably. Only Placido remained silent. It was a wonder that Dancy was still alive.
Staked out as he was in the blistering hot sun like a
wild animal, no doubt with little food or water, and
the target of contempt and brutality from all Comancheros—men, women and children alike—the
lawman had to admit that Will Dancy was a hell of
a lot better man than he'd figured.

As he watched, two more Comancheros crossed
to the pump, had their drink, and then removing
their broad, rolled brim hats, took turns lowering
their heads and holding them under the pump
spout while water was gushed down upon them.

Several women laughing, shouting and talking
back and forth, dressed as were most in shirtwaist
and full skirt, circled past Dancy on their way to
the main house. All slowed when they were
abreast, some taunting him with words and flash-

ing displays of their bare legs, others kicking dirt or picking up some of the rocks scattered about and hurling them at the Ranger. Through it all Dancy showed no reaction—not even when one of the younger-looking ones scooped up a handful of mud from alongside the trough and threw it into his sun-darkened face.

Abruptly a half a dozen riders raced into the camp. Halting at one of the hitch racks, they dismounted, hurried up to Hacho, and began to speak.

"You recognize the one doing the talking?" Rye said, directing his question to both Ligon and Placido.

"*Sí, jefe,*" Placido replied. "He is the one we did not kill on the Rio Grande."

"Yes, sir, he's the stinking sonofabitch that got away from us," Ligon said. "Thought he looked familiar."

"Hacho probably sent him and that bunch back to look for us—"

"Name's Gatillo," Ligon said. "Heard him called that when they was tying me up. He's sort of a second leader."

"A sub-chief," Placido said. "There are many of them in Hacho's army."

Gatillo was a small, wiry man in dirty white pants, blue shirt and large straw hat, also decorated with silver. He wore the customary crossed bandoleros as well as two revolvers and a long knife. The distance was too great for Rye to get a good look at the man's features, but he appeared to be young.

"Probably telling Hacho that he couldn't find no

sign of us," Ligon said, "if like you say, he's been out looking for us."

"That'd be my guess," Rye said, brushing at the moisture blurring his vision. The heat still held and he felt as if his entire body were clothed with sweat.

The digging about in the pile of clothing on the porch had ended. Several of the women, carrying what they had chosen, began to head back across the hardpack for their huts. They appeared to have been rewarded with only articles of clothing, cooking utensils and other household pieces. Rye reckoned that all other items—guns, silverware, money, and the like that were of value—had already been claimed by the Comanchero leader and divided between him and his men, with Hacho, of course, getting the lion's share.

The sun finally began to drop below the ragged rim of the Sierra Madre. Shadows were lengthening and the heat, at last, seemed to be diminishing; but it would be hours yet before coolness set in, Rye knew.

"One of them's coming up the hill," Ligon warned suddenly in a low voice.

Rye turned just in time to see the Comanchero, a bottle of liquor of some kind in his hand, move unsteadily away from the crowd on the hardpack and start up the hill.

"I will go to meet him," Placido said quietly. "It is all right?"

"Go ahead," Rye answered, "but no shooting."

Placido patted the knife hanging from his belt. "Do not worry, *jefe*. The blade makes no sound."

Rye watched the Comanchero begin a faltering

ascent of the steep slope, stumbling, clawing at the clumps of chaparral and jojoba to keep from falling, all the while holding the bottle of liquor above at arm's length to prevent its being smashed against the gravelly surface. Halfway up the man went down. Muttering, he drew himself to his knees and then erect. Lips still twisting with angry words, he stood for a long minute swaying uncertainly, and then coming to a decision, turned and started back down the grade.

Rye breathed easier. That Placido could take care of the outlaw without using his gun was a certainty, but the man could have managed to cry out or otherwise do something that would attract attention of someone down on the hardpack was very possible.

Placido, his features expressionless, crawled back to his place beside Ligon. The ex-Ranger swore. "Sure am glad that's over. Was afeared a tussle would give us away."

Placido shook his head. "A throat cut cannot make sound, *señor*," he said with a half smile.

"No, I reckon it can't, but maybe he'd kick some rocks loose, or rattle the brush—something like that."

Rye was only half listening, his attention again on the activity on the hardpack. A fire was being built out in its center, fueled by brush brought up from the river and by the unwanted leftover articles taken in the raid. As the sun sank lower and the heat broke slightly, more people appeared, some coming from the huts, others from the main house. Bottles of liquor were to be seen in the hands of several—wine, tequila, aguardiente, even tizwin, according to Placido—but as yet there was no drunkenness.

"Celebrating something," Ligon said. "The raid, I expect."

Rye nodded. "About it."

Ligon rubbed at his whiskered jaw. "Sure hope they don't decide to make Will a part of it."

"I'm hoping that, too," Rye said, glancing to the west. "Soon as it's a mite darker, we'll get the horses and circle around to where we'll be closer to him. If they do start something with him maybe we'll be able to step in and bale him out."

"There's a lot of them down there," Ligon murmured.

"Know that. Let's just do like I'm saying—get around to the other side and lay low. Could be they'll leave him be."

CHAPTER 9

Small fires began to appear here and there in front of the huts. Women could be seen working around them, suspending kettles over the flames, and flattening out corn cakes into tortillas on nearby rocks and then setting them to bake. The odors of cooking mutton and chile began to permeate the warm air, stirring hunger pangs within Rye and the men.

But there would be no evening meal for them—at least for a while. Later, after they had moved to the opposite side of the hardpack, and were closer to Will Dancy, they could make a supper of dried meat and hard biscuits. They would have to forego coffee and all other items in their grub sacks that required a fire.

The day slid gradually into sunset. The sky above the Sierra Madre faded into pale yellow, and then gold, finally darkening to gray. Someone down in the camp started plucking a guitar. Several of the women, not abandoning their cooking chores, began to sing. A number of dogs, content to lie in the shadows of the huts and larger buildings during the day when the heat was at its worst, had been roused by the smells of meat and other edibles, and could now be seen prowling lethargically about.

A man came out of the main house where smoke

was twisting slowly up from the chimney, and set a pan of food alongside Will Dancy. From the distance Rye and the others could not determine what the meal consisted of, but the Ranger fell upon it with gusto and quickly ate all that had been placed before him.

"Treating him like he was one of them dogs," Ligon grumbled. "Hell, there ain't one of them fit to lick his boots!"

"Whatever they're feeding him he seems to like," Rye commented.

"It will be meat and chile and such things," Placido said. "Hacho wishes to keep him well for the day when he will make great sport with him. A strong man can endure more and thus provide much merriment."

Ligon wagged his head. "The Mexican people are mighty fine folks. One of these days they're going to get up on their hind legs and go after these Comancheros themselves—do the job the army's supposed to do."

"It is a matter of fear, *señor*," Placido said. "It will come when something arouses courage and fear is forgotten."

The big fire lighting up the yard fronting the main house and huts, fed continually by the Comancheros, burned brightly. The evening meal over men began to appear, some with a jug or bottle of wine or liquor of some kind in hand, and made their way to the main house where some entered while others contented themselves with sitting down on the porch, shoulders pressed against the wall.

More riders came in, their horses stirring up a

cloud of dust that drifted over the hardpack and mingled with the smoke, which brought several shrill complaints from women still engaged in cooking.

"If this here's Hacho's main camp and he's hanging around all the time, why hasn't the army raided it and put an end to him and his bunch?" Rye wondered.

"They have tried—many times, I think," Placido said. "But Hacho has the cunning of a coyote. He and his men are always gone when the soldiers come. They find only the women and the villagers who refused to leave their homes when the Comancheros came."

"Couldn't they tell the soldiers where—"

"They tell nothing, *jefe*. They are much afraid of what will happen to them if they talk to the soldiers. Also, they know that Hacho will not remain long. He will move to a new camp when it becomes too dangerous to stay in the old one."

Rye shrugged. He had encountered similar situations along the frontier on his own side of the border—instances where a powerful rancher or landowner had held a small settlement captive through fear and force.

"If the Rangers and the *Federales* could ever get together they maybe could do something about Hacho and his kind," Ligon said. "But, no—they've got to spend their time chasing each other back and forth across the border."

"It is said they cannot ever be friends," Placido added. "And such are words I believe. I have heard the soldiers talk. There is a hate for the Rangers, for lawmen of all kinds north of the border."

"Might as well just say for all *gringos*," Hugh Ligon said with a shrug.

Placido's expression did not change as he stared down into the Comanchero camp. "Yes, but I do not like the word. I have many friends on the other side of the Rio Grande and I will not degrade them with such a word—although there are some who deserve to be called such. But it is sad the Rangers and the soldiers cannot ride together and kill off Hacho and men like him. It is my thought that only a man alone, or perhaps two, such as you, can ever accomplish the deed."

"Expect you've tried many times—"

"It has not been as often as I would wish. I have my wife, my children, and Hacho, as I have said, moves to new camps. He has stayed in Vado longer than usual. But to kill him is like to kill a scorpion. There are many more who will take his place."

"Like Gatillo," Ligon said.

"*Sí*, like him."

"Makes it sound pretty hopeless," Rye said. "Like this country will never be rid of his kind."

"It is possible but I doubt there will ever be another with the cunning and cruel ways of Hacho. Perhaps if he dies the new leader will be one the soldiers can quickly overcome and thus bring about an end to this party as well to the others."

Rye glanced to the sky. It was darkening but there were few clouds, and the moon and stars, now beginning to make their presence known, would brighten the land. They could use a dark night, he thought, but long ago he'd learned a man could not always have things the way he wanted them: that he simply played the cards dealt him, as wisely as he could.

Only a few of the small cooking fires still burned and the number of loungers on the porch of the main house had increased. Women no longer sang but the guitar player still plucked the strings of his instrument. A dog yelped in pain as someone kicked or struck it, and the good odor of chile and meat, and other food cooking, had now been crowded out by smoke and the rank smells of burning creosote bush and other brush assisted by paper, clothing, bits of broken furniture, and other unwanted articles from the raid.

Lamps began to glow in the windows of the main house, while candles and an occasional lantern lit up some of the huts. The old church, too, showed some activity, not of a religious nature but as living quarters for a number of the outlaw band.

Hacho, in company with three of his men—one of whom was Gatillo—came out onto the porch of the main house and paused at its forward edge. All were smoking cigars and one had a bottle of wine or some other liquor, from which he took a swallow at regular intervals. Hacho and the others did not share the bottle—something that Rye and Hugh Ligon took note of.

"I figured they'd all be getting drunk," the one-time Ranger said. "Sort of counted on it—would've made it easier to cut Will loose."

Rye agreed, but again it was a matter beyond his control and he wasted no time regretting it.

The bonfire near the center of the hardpack continued to burn brightly. It threw a broad flare of yellow and orange in a wide circle, and touched the fronts of the huts with flickering light. One of the women suddenly appeared from the shadows, and swirling her full skirt, began to dance. Men sprawled about on the cooling hardpack, and on the porch, started a rhythmic clapping. The guitar player forsaking his solo attempts, turned his talents to accompanying the onlookers.

Shortly another woman joined the first, and then a third came onto the scene. At that point several men got to their feet and joined in, some dancing, some singing, others merely continuing the clapping. Hacho and the Comancheros with him, strolled to the end of the porch, and still puffing on their cigars, watched. More men and women appeared in the yard, coming from the huts, the main house and the church, all taking up various positions in the circular flare of the bonfire.

Rye groaned and lay back on the weedy surface of the hilltop. They could do nothing until the Comancheros returned to their quarters and retired— and the way it looked at that moment he, Ligon, and Placido had a long wait ahead of them.

CHAPTER 10

The last of the cooking fires had long since died out and the community bonfire was now little more than glowing embers. Most of the Comancheros and their women had retired to their quarters, the only ones still to be seen were a half dozen or so stretched out on the porch of the main house apparently sleeping soundly. Dogs still nosed around the now-quiet yard searching for scraps of food, and the only sound to be heard was the hooting of a lonely owl along the river.

Rye had watched until the last of the huts went dark, and then got to his feet. "Let's move out," he said, and then added to Ligon, "Best you quiet those spurs."

Ligon and Placido had risen immediately at the marshal's words. The one-time Ranger hurriedly bent down, and taking up two small twigs, wedged them in between the rowels and the frame of the spurs.

"I reckon that'll do it," he said, stamping his feet.

It had grown steadily cooler as the night aged, and a chill now filled the air. The desert, ever fickle and as deadly in the day as it was beautiful at night, could turn brutally cold after the sun was gone.

"When do we get Will?" Ligon asked as they descended the slope to the cluster of trees where they had picketed the horses.

"Have to get set first," Rye answered. "We'll not have a second chance. We make one slip-up and we'll have the whole camp down on us plenty fast."

They reached the horses, freed the reins and mounted up. The land before them lay in moon and starlight bathed silence, and touching the chestnut lightly with his blunted spurs, Rye headed west for a hundred yards or so and then cut left. Following a wide curve they came in finally to the corrals standing to the south of the main house. The marshal considered the line of brush and timber boxed in affairs for a brief time, and then rode on to the one farthest east, and halted.

"We'll be needing a horse for Dancy," he said to Placido as they all came off the saddle. He pointed to one of the makeshift enclosure in which a dozen or so mounts, still with gear, were standing slack hipped in the pale light. "Get one of those. Won't have to bother with saddling or bridling him."

Placido nodded, and gathering in the lines of their three horses, moved up to the gate of the corral. Securing the animals to a nearby clump, he turned to Rye.

"It is here that I am to wait for you?"

"Right here—with the extra horse," Rye said in a low voice. "If we're lucky we'll be back with Dancy. If you hear shooting, best you climb on your pony and get away fast."

Placido shrugged. "I could be of help, *jefe*—"

"Know that," the lawman said, "but it'll be better if you stay right here and have the horses ready.

If it turns out we can't free Dancy, one more man with us won't help."

Ligon listening in silence, rubbed his jaw. "John, you're talking like we ain't got much of a chance to do what we're figuring on."

Rye's shoulders stirred slightly. "This is one time I rate the maybes a couple of notches below the likelys. You ready?"

"Ready as I'll ever be," Ligon replied drawing his gun.

Rye shook his head and pointed to the knife hanging at the ex-Ranger's side. "That's what you'll be needing—not that six-shooter. One shot's all it will take to get us chained to that post along with Dancy."

Ligon nodded his understanding and slid the weapon back into the holster and drew the long-bladed knife. Moonlight glinted off its steel surface.

"Long time since I used this on a man," he murmured.

"With a little luck you won't have to now," Rye said, and keeping in the shadows along the make-shift corrals, moved off toward the yard.

Reaching the end of the enclosures, he halted. Raising himself to where he could see the huts and the front of the main house, he gave them careful study. There was no sign of anyone being up and abroad.

"Stay low," he warned Ligon, and hunched, crossed to the near corner of the main house.

Again Rye paused and made a close check of the premises. The porch, with its several sleeping outlaws, was visible to him now and for a long minute he considered the recumbent figures. Finally con-

vinced there would be no trouble from that source
—at least for the time being—he transferred his attention once more to the shacks. He stiffened.
Reaching back he touched Ligon on the arm. One
of the Comancheros had abruptly appeared in the
entrance to a nearby hut.

Rye tensed. The outlaw, if it was a drink of water
he sought, would cross to the pump, following a
course that would take him alongside the main
house. The lawman moved back slowly, quietly, re-
treating into the shadows with Ligon. Drawing his
knife he waited, poised, ready to strike swiftly and
silently should the man veer and pass by too close.

Taut, body like a coiled spring needing only a
touch to be released, Rye watched the outlaw. The
man stood motionless for several minutes, staring
off into the silvered desert beyond the camp. Taking a sack of tobacco from the pocket of his dark
shirt, he detached a single sheet of thin paper from
the pack attached to it, held it partly folded between thumb and forefinger, poured a small quantity of tobacco into the waiting cylinder, and skill-
fully rolled himself a cigarette.

That accomplished the Comanchero hung the
smoke in a corner of his mouth, returned the sack
of tobacco—no doubt once the property of some
luckless pilgrim who had fallen victim during a
raid—to his pocket. Crossing leisurely then to the
almost lifeless remains of the bonfire, he picked up
a glowing brand, and holding it to the tip of the
cigarette, puffed it into life. Tossing the brand back
into the ashes, the outlaw turned his attention toward the corrals, smoke drifting lazily away from
him in thin, intermittent clouds as the coal at the

tip of the cigarette alternately glowed and went dark in rhythm with his puffing.

Rye's eyes narrowed as he strained to see. Had the man spotted Placido? Did he suspect something was wrong?

Ligon's thoughts were apparently along the same line. "He's a dead one if he goes back to that corral," he said softly.

Rye nodded. Placido could be depended upon to handle the outlaw—but there was always the chance the man might manage to yell, to cry out and send out an alarm. If he—

The Comanchero wheeled suddenly and began to make his way back to the hut. Reaching the entrance to the wood and adobe structure he hesitated, flipped the still glowing cigarette off into the yard, and then entered.

Rye felt tension flow from his tall frame. Hugh Ligon sighed audibly.

"Was close. I figured we had trouble."

"Same here," the marshal said, and glancing about added, "Come on—let's get done with this."

They crossed quickly to the pump and horse trough. Crouched there in its shadow Rye and Ligon waited out another dragging minute, and then bent low, moved to where Dancy lay. Putting his hand over the Ranger's mouth to stifle any possible cry of surprise or alarm, Rye nodded to Ligon.

"Cut the belt. It's the only way we'll get him loose."

Dancy, eyes wide, stared up at the marshal. Rye removed his hand as Ligon began to sever the thick leather strap that encircled the Ranger's waist.

"It's Hugh Ligon and me—John Rye," the lawman said. "We're here to get you."

Dancy's mouth tightened and a look of relief came over his sun-browned features. "Been hoping —praying. Had about give up. There just the two of you?"

"Got the breed—Placido—waiting with the horses," Ligon replied. "There, the belt's cut. You're loose, Will."

Dancy sat up immediately and glanced around. "Sure some surprise," he said, fixing his eyes on Rye. "Never figured to get any help from the great Doomsday Marshal."

The thread of sarcasm in Dancy's tone was undeniable. Rye smiled tightly. Will Dancy hadn't changed, that was certain.

"Best we get the hell out of here fast," he said stiffly. "Some of that bunch on the porch could wake up."

"For sure," Ligon said, pulling Dancy to his feet.

They crossed the yard and reached the corner of the main house with Rye in the lead. Moving hurriedly, but quietly, they covered the distance along the structure's side to its rear. There Dancy came to a stop.

"What's the matter, Will?" Ligon asked in a puzzled voice.

Rye halted, half-turned. "What's the matter. "We're taking a big chance—"

Dancy rubbed at the whiskers on his face and shook his head. "I'm obliged to you both, but I can't leave."

"Can't!" Rye echoed in a husky voice. "Why the

hell can't you? After going through what we have and—"

"There's four women being held prisoner inside the house," Dancy cut in. "All Americans, just like us. I can't go off and leave them knowing what they're up against."

CHAPTER 11

"Women!" Ligon echoed. "White women?"

"Yeah, were took captive by Hacho and his damned renegades."

"Expect he's aiming to sell them to some fancy house—"

"The ones in Chihuahua. Does a big business with them. One of the women is just a kid about fifteen or sixteen. Blonde hair, kind of like gold, and has blue eyes. She's about the prettiest thing I've ever seen. Hacho's holding her special. Won't let any of his bunch even get near her. Figures to get a real high price for her."

"What about the others?" Ligon asked.

"Ain't none of them what you'd call old, they just ain't young like Ida Lee—that's her name—and they've all been married. Expect they'll fetch a good price, all right, but nothing like that Ida Lee will bring. She's only been here a week or so. Said they'd killed both her pa and ma."

Dancy, showing the effects of the inactivity that being chained to a post brought about, leaned up against the side of the building. "I sure ain't got much steam," he murmured, and brushed at his face.

"The rest of the women must have had kinfolk, too," Rye said. "Know what happened to them?"

"Murdered them from what I heard."

"Thought they made captives of the men and then sold them out to work in the mines," Rye said. Having four women along would not only hinder them as they made a run for the border with Will Dancy, but would more than double the danger. They could expect the Comancheros to be on their trail immediately after discovering that Dancy was missing. With the women also gone, especially the young one Hacho considered his prize, they would intensify their efforts to stop them.

"They do, if they're young enough to stand up under such hard labor," Dancy said, answering Rye's comment. "Now, I want you to know I'm mighty obliged to you for coming here after me, but you go right ahead and head back to the border without me, if you're of a mind. I can't go and leave those women here knowing what's ahead for them —and taking them along will sure slow you down. You just give me a knife and gun—"

Rye shook his head. Dancy was mistaking his concern for a reluctance to help the women. "We won't be leaving here without them," he said. "Where are they?"

Relief was evident on the Ranger's features. "Inside the house. Got them locked in a corner room."

"You see them there?" Ligon asked.

"No, but the one named Arabella Simpson said a few words to me one time when they was all at the pump. The Comancheros' women bring them out once a day, all tied together with a rope, and let them wash up and drink. She told me they were being kept in that back corner room, and if I ever got a chance to help them I'd know where they

were. I never figured I'd get the chance, that I'd
likely be dead before that happened."

"They abuse them much?" Ligon wanted to
know.

"Can't say, Hugh. I'm for certain none of them
have laid a hand on Ida Lee, and if they have any of
the others I expect they're too ashamed to own up
to it. Now, if we're going to do something, we best
get at it. Morning ain't far off—get's light early
around here, and we're sure going to be needing a
good start."

Ligon glanced at Rye. The marshal's attention
was on one of the huts where candlelight now
showed in its open doorway.

"What about it, John? Are we aiming to—"

Rye nodded, and brought his glance back to
Dancy. "Do you know exactly where the women
are and how to get to them?"

The Ranger shook his head. "All I know is that
they're in that far corner room."

"You can't say if there're guards or not?"

"Arabella said Hacho keeps a man at the door to
the room. Job is to stop any of the bunch that gets
ideas about the women from going in."

"Who else is sleeping in the building? Must be
some others."

"You're right. The men who ain't married or
don't have a woman bunk in the rooms—I think
there are six or eight of them. And Hacho and his
woman's in there somewhere, most likely in the
front."

Will Dancy knew very little about the interior of
the main house other than the fact that the women
were being held prisoner in a room at the northeast

corner of the structure, and that a guard was posted at the entrance to their quarters. What the arrangements were insofar as the Comancheros who also occupied the building was unknown and anybody's guess. But the women had to be helped—he didn't need Will Dancy to tell him that.

"How do we get inside the place—do you know that?"

Dancy stiffened slightly at the marshal's tone. "There's a back door. Can see it from the corrals. I don't know exactly what it opens into, a hall, I suspect, as that's the way they build houses around here."

"The rooms could all lead off a hall, and the one the women is in likely's at the far end," Ligon said.

"We'll have to take a chance on that being the way of it," Rye said, and started for the corner of the building.

Reaching there, he glanced along the east wall of the house. The door that Dancy mentioned was near the center of the building. At that moment Placido appeared, moving like a wisp of smoke in the pale light.

"The horses, they are by the last corral—"

"Good," Rye said, nodding. "We'll be needing four more."

"Four more, *jefe, por que*—why?"

"Hacho's got four women they've captured. We're taking them back with us."

"If we can get them out of that house," Ligon said, showing doubt for the first time. "Sure going to be a mighty touchy thing."

"Such is true," Placido agreed, adding, "I will

have the horses ready. Do you wish me to go with you into the house?"

"No," Rye replied, "it's best you stay with the horses. The whole thing could go for nothing if we got the women out and then didn't have any horses to ride."

"*Sí, jefe,*" Placido said, clearly disappointed. Abruptly he came to attention. "Someone comes."

Rye swore softly. With so many Comancheros in the camp they could expect to run up against one or more at any given moment.

"Get down," he said quietly and dropped to a crouch.

The scuff of boot heels on the hard, baked ground broke the hush. It was a sound that had failed to register on his hearing moments earlier. Placido's sense of awareness was far more acute than his even though he'd trained himself for just such times, the marshal realized.

"Two men. They come to the corrals," Placido murmured.

"Aiming to have a look at the horses," Ligon said in a low voice. "They'll spot ours for damn sure."

"We've got time to move back into the shadows a mite," Dancy suggested. "Good chance they won't see us there."

"Too risky—moving about," Rye said. "Just stay down. I'll give Placido a hand."

"No, it is for me, *jefe,*" Placido said, and close to the ground, moved silently off along the edge of the corral.

Placido's hatred for the Comancheros was going to get him killed some day, Rye thought, and ignoring the half-breed's words, took his knife in his right hand, his .45, held club fashion, in the left, and moved off after the man.

Over on the far side of the camp a dog began to bark, the noise breaking the quiet. Whether the racket would arouse some of the Comancheros the lawman could only guess. He halted. Placido, a dim shape in the shadowy night, was just ahead. He had stopped at the corner of the corral, was crouched against the unstable wall of brush and vines. The sounds of the approaching outlaws had grown louder in the tense silence, and the odor of the cigars or cigarettes they were smoking was now more pronounced on the warm air.

Placido twisted about and faced Rye. In the night his features were dark and sharply chiseled. Pointing to himself he raised the knife he was holding and indicated he would step out ahead of Rye and strike down the nearest outlaw. It would be up to the marshal to take care of the other. The lawman nodded his understanding. He had no liking for using a knife in such moments, always preferring his .45, but keeping things quiet was a matter of most importance.

The dog had ceased its barking, and the scrape of boot heels and jingle of spurs was now close. Both Rye and Placido drew up tight, prepared to lunge forward and strike swiftly. Abruptly the Comancheros reached the end of the corral. One was wearing his large, rolled brim *sombrero* pushed to the back of his head, the other, a taller man, had left his hat behind.

Suddenly Placido, with the quiet speed of a striking rattlesnake, hurled himself at the nearest outlaw. Moonlight glittered on the blade in his hand as it arced upward and then came down. In that same instant John Rye also threw himself upon the Comanchero directly before him.

"Ai-i-eee!" the man cried out as the blade drove into his chest. "*Madre de Dios — I—*"

Rye's hand clamped over the outlaw's mouth even as he was falling. Nearby Placido had silently and efficiently disposed of his objective, and was now standing over the outlaw's lifeless shape.

The marshal, allowing the body of the man he was holding to sink to the ground, looked anxiously toward the hardpack. He had stifled the yell that had risen in the outlaw's throat before it was well started, but there had been some sound—enough that anyone listening could have heard.

For several valuable minutes the lawman remained motionless listening into the night. Finally, when there was no indication that the half-cry of the man had been noticed, he drew himself fully upright, and motioning to Placido, returned to where Ligon and Will Dancy waited.

"You think anybody might have heard that jasper yell?" Ligon asked at once. "Weren't much but—"

"We waited to see but nobody showed up," Rye said. He paused as Dancy moved past him and hurried to where the two outlaws lay. Kneeling, he drew the knife from one of the dead Comanchero's belt and thrust it under his own.

"They ain't carrying no guns," he said as he retraced his steps to the others. "I reckon this toad-stabber'll just have to do me."

Rye turned to Placido. "Four more horses, that's what we'll be needing. And we'll meet you right here. Understand?"

"*Sí, jefe,*" Placido answered in a low voice. That he was pleased at the outcome of the encounter with the two Comancheros was evident in his tone. "They will be ready. But first I will move the dead *asesinos* off into the brush where they will not be found."

Placido was right. Other members of Hacho's band might come out to have a look at the horses and discover the bodies of the dead men.

Rye nodded his approval and came about. "You ready?" he asked, facing Ligon and Dancy.

"Sure am," Will Dancy said, and keeping in the shadows, led the way to the rear entrance of the Comanchero house.

CHAPTER 12

The door stood partly open. The men stepped quietly into the hallway to which it led and came to a halt, momentarily stalled by the stench of sweat, unwashed bodies, rotting food and spilled liquor.

In the dim confines of the narrow hallway Rye strained to make out the exact arrangement. There were several rooms lying along its length, he saw. Faint sounds of snoring were coming from the nearest. Moving up to it the marshal paused.

There was no wooden door, only a heavy drapery that had been pulled aside to admit air. The room was in darkness except for thin shreds of moonlight struggling through a dust covered window in the south wall. All was indistinct but Rye was able to distinguish a solitary bed upon which four or perhaps five men lay. Others sprawled about on blankets on the floor while still others were getting their night's rest on a ragged-looking old mattress.

Nine, possibly ten men in that one room. Figuring the same number in the remainder of quarters —excluding the room the women were being held captive in, and the one being occupied by the Comanchero leader himself, would mean there were in the neighborhood of three dozen outlaws in the adobe building. Add to that the men who could be found on the porch and in the different huts and the church, and the total of Comancheros in the camp would reach at least seventy, probably more.

Safely past the first room, Rye turned to Dancy. "You said the women were in the corner of the building. That means they'll be in the last room on our right."

In the same low whisper, Dancy said, "I guess so."

Guess so! Rye cursed silently. Standing there in the center of a house full of murderous renegades guessing could get them all killed.

"Was what you said earlier," Ligon reminded Dancy.

"It's where they are," the Ranger whispered. "Got to studying on it later, after I said it, and wasn't sure if the woman said right or left. Was right. Know that now."

Rye nodded. "Hacho?"

"Don't know about him. In one of the front rooms I expect. Why? You going in after him, too?"

"No, only the women. Just trying to get everything straight in my mind," he replied quietly, and started on down the corridor.

Carefully, listening intently, Rye moved on with Dancy and Ligon at his heels. The second room had no bed, he saw as they drew abreast. The outlaws were scattered about on the floor, some using blankets as a mat, others simply sleeping on the bare wood. He found the situation to be the same in the room opposite.

One of the dogs set up a furious barking somewhere outside, near one of the corrals. At once he

drew up against the wall, motioning for Ligon and
Dancy to do likewise. If the noise roused one of the
Comancheros in the house and he decided to inves-
tigate, they would be in for a confrontation. Rye
thought fast, considered what they should do in
such event. Spread out—that was it. Have Ligon
and Dancy each cover two of the doorways, he
would look after three. If an outlaw appeared in
any one of them he would have to be dispatched
quickly and silently so as none of the remaining
Comancheros would take notice.

Rye motioned Ligon and Dancy to their positions along the hall. If the dog aroused the Comancheros it would be a different story; there'd be no
necessity for the silence of a knife; sixguns would
be in order, and with their use he and the two men
with him would quickly be confronted by the rest
of the camp.

With that would come the realization they had
accomplished nothing in their efforts to rescue Will
Dancy other than ridding the country of a few Comancheros, and getting themselves killed in the
shootout. But what the hell! A man couldn't expect
to live forever—and what better way to die than
with a gun in his hand doing what he figured was
right?

The dog yelped and suddenly stopped barking.
There had been no sign of anyone inside the house
taking notice. Apparently it was a man from one of
the huts that had silenced him—or it could have
been Placido. Rye drew a deep breath, glanced at
Dancy and Hugh Ligon. The release of the tension
that had gripped them was evident in the relaxing
of their shoulders.

"Goddamned dog," Ligon murmured.

Rye grinned at the old Ranger's heartfelt words, and continued along the corridor, taking each step with care, wincing visibly when a board beneath his booted feet squeaked. The huts would all have dirt floors; he could only wish that this building had been similarly equipped.

The last two rooms, the one in which it was thought Hacho occupied was just ahead on his left, the one in which the women were being held was opposite on the right. There was a chair placed in front of the latter, shut off from the hallway by a thick mat of reeds. A like arrangement shielded the Comanchero chief's quarters.

Rye drew his .45. Gripping it by the barrel, he made ready to use it as a club. Both Ligon and Dancy, pulling up behind him, held their knives in a striking position.

"I don't like this," the marshal muttered as they halted. "Chair's here for the guard. Where is he?"

"Supposed to be setting here keeping his *compadres* away from the women," Dancy said in a whisper. "My guess is he ain't far."

"Maybe he's inside," Ligon suggested.

"Or maybe gone to get himself a drink," the Ranger said, and moving past John Rye, pushed aside the reed curtain and eased quietly into the room.

Rye followed immediately, keeping to Dancy's left shoulder. Ligon, moonlight glinting off his knife blade, was close behind.

"Ladies," Dancy called softly. "We're Americans. We're here to get you out of here."

There was a slight rustling over in the southwest

corner of the room. Rye tensed. For some reason he thought the women would be on the opposite side.

"You hear? We're friends. We're here to help you," Dancy continued in the same low, cautious tone. "I'm the man they had chained out by the pump. My friends came to get me. We decided to take you with us."

"Oh, God!" a woman's voice, filled with relief, murmured. "Oh, thank God!"

"You'll need to be real quiet," Rye warned. "We're a long way from being—"

In that fleeting moment the marshal saw a shadowy figure lunge at Dancy from the corner where the rustling noise had sounded. The guard! As he saw Will Dancy wheel to meet the Comanchero, he glimpsed a second figure in the dimness rushing toward him. Instinctively he rocked to one side and lashed out with the gun he was holding. There was a dull thud as the heavy weapon smashed into bone, and then a limp body fell against his legs and slid to the floor. Gun raised to strike again if necessary, Rye looked down. His mouth tightened. It was one of the Comanchero women.

At that moment he felt Dancy come up against him. His first thought was that the Ranger was hurt, that the Comanchero not wanting to risk a gunshot for fear of awakening Hacho and other members of the band, thus revealing not only his incompetence but that he was passing his time with a woman, had driven his knife into Dancy. But the Ranger's voice was strong as he spoke.

"Help me lay this jasper down. Don't want him making any noise falling."

"He dead?" Ligon asked.

"Expect he is. Put my knife clean through him," Dancy said laconically.

Rye reached past the Ranger and caught the outlaw, a large, heavy man, by the arm and assisted Dancy in lowering the dead man to the floor.

"Let's drag him over to where he was," Rye said, and taking one of the Comanchero's arms while Dancy grasped the other, they pulled the inert body back to the corner of the room and laid it out on the mattress that was there.

"What about that'n you tangled with?" the Ranger asked. "He dead, too?"

"Not sure. It's a woman not a man," Rye said as they hurriedly returned to where the crumpled shape lay. He bent over her, felt for a pulse. "She's alive. We'll have to gag and tie her up."

"Hell, she's just as bad as Hacho and the rest! Why not stick a knife in her, too? Be less trouble."

"Maybe so, but that's not to my liking," Rye said coolly. "I'll see to her while you and Ligon get the women ready to move out."

The Comanchero woman's shirtwaist was unbuttoned and hanging open. Taking it in his hands the marshal ripped it off and tore it into three strips after which he carried the senseless form to the mattress, where he tied one strip tightly over the woman's mouth, and used the others to bind her hands and feet. The lawman worked rapidly, making every moment count, acutely conscious of passing time. They had already been inside the Comanchero headquarters—evidently once the home of a wealthy Mexican family who had been dispossessed and probably slain by Hacho and his renegades—far too long, and every second was now loaded with danger.

Finished, Rye wheeled and returned to the center of the room. "We've got to get out of here—"

"We're ready," a woman's voice cut in. "Even took off our shoes so we wouldn't make any noise walking."

"That's good," Rye said, turning to the doorway. "We've got to go down the hall and Hacho's men are asleep in rooms on both sides."

"We know," the woman said. "You can depend on us doing just what you tell us to do. Myrtle, I want you to help me with Dora."

"Sure," another female voice answered.

"Best you put your arm around her to keep her walking straight. I'll hold my hand over her mouth so's she won't say something, or yell out like she sometimes does. Wait for just a mite."

Rye, standing in the doorway, saw the woman cross to the west wall of the room and take up the rifle the guard had propped against its plastered surface.

"Just maybe'll need this," she said, and glancing at the dead outlaw on the mattress nearby, spat on him. "Feel better now," she added and hurried to rejoin the others waiting just inside the doorway.

Rye turned his attention to Ligon and Will Dancy standing in the hall. "All clear?"

"All clear," Ligon said.

CHAPTER 13

Drawing back a step, Rye nodded to Ligon. "You and Dancy go ahead with the women," he said in a low whisper. "I'll bring up the rear—just in case any of the outlaws wake up. If they do—don't stop, keep going."

Ligon murmured. "I savvy," and, relaying the marshal's words to the Ranger, started off along the hallway with the women following silently.

They reached the entrance to the first room and paused while Dancy had a quick look inside. In the half dark Rye saw him beckon, an indication that it was safe to proceed. At once the party resumed its slow, careful passage along the corridor.

Rye began to move, gun in one hand, knife ready in the other. Coming to the first doorway, he also halted and had his look into the evil-smelling, crowded room. There was no sign of any of the outlaws being awake, as Dancy had found, and pressed quietly on.

Up ahead Ligon and Dancy were leading the women past the last room and were now moving through the outer doorway into the open. Rye quickened his steps, and then in a small, tight group they hurriedly crossed to the shadows lying alongside the corrals and made their way to where Placido was to meet them.

The night had turned cold, as is typical of the desert, and one of the women began to shiver. Ligon removed his leather vest and handed it to her.

"Got a brush jacket tied to my saddle," the one-time Ranger said. "You can put it on when we get to the horses."

Rye looked on beyond the two men and the women, the horses—where were they? Where was Placido? They were at the place where—

Will Dancy, leading the party, came to a halt. He raised his hand for silence. Immediately Rye hurried to the Ranger's side.

"What is it?"

"Heard something—or somebody, over toward that last hut," Dancy said in a low voice.

Rye stared off into the direction indicated. He could see no signs of movement, but he knew a man like Dancy would not be one to err at such moments.

"*Jefe*—"

At the sound of Placido's soft call, Rye swung his attention to a stand of brush growing near the corral a few steps ahead.

"Yeh, Placido?"

"It is best you wait," Placido said. "A man and his woman—they are walking about."

"Quick—everybody up against the side of the corral so's you'll be in the dark," the marshal said tautly. "No talking or moving about."

Before he had finished his muted order the women and Hugh Ligon had done as directed. Dancy, crouched beside him, half turned.

"I'll take care of them—"

Rye dropped a hand on the Ranger's shoulder. "Wait. Could be it won't be necessary. They might not come this way, and we'd be fools to risk a ruckus that just might bring the whole camp down on us."

Dancy muttered something inaudible, and then in a stronger, exasperated tone added, "Man ought to kill a goddamn Comanchero any time he gets the chance. The sooner we rid this country of them, the better for everybody."

"I agree," Rye said quietly, "at least to the last part of it. But we're a long way from the border and we can't take any unnecessary chances or—"

The lawman broke off. He saw the outlaw couple in that moment. They appeared to be arguing as they walked slowly along—and they were moving directly toward the end of the last corral where Placido was to have the horses waiting.

The voices of the Comanchero and his woman, quick and angry words, grew louder. Rye saw Will Dancy draw himself up as if, regardless of the marshal's cautioning, he intended to follow through with his threat.

"I ain't caring," the Ranger said. "I owe them for what they done to me—and I ain't letting them catch me alive. If something gets started, you and the others ride on."

Rye could not blame Dancy for the way he felt. His time as a prisoner of the Comancheros would have been hell at its worst, but Rye could not afford to let the vengeance ravaging the Ranger endanger the others in the party. They had been lucky so far, had only to wait until the outlaw and his woman turned back, or drew close enough to where they could be taken care of without arousing other Comancheros.

"Just back off, Will. Let Placido handle it," he said softly.

Abruptly the couple halted. More heated words were exchanged. The crack of flesh meeting flesh sounded as one of the pair slapped the other. A moment later Rye saw the dim outline of the woman as she hurried angrily off in the direction of one of the huts.

He could not see the Comanchero, his view being blocked now by the side of the brush corral, but there was the faint crunch of boots on sand as the man continued his stroll.

"He's aiming to look at the horses," Dancy muttered. "Still figure I best—"

"No, we'll leave it up to Placido," the marshal said, repeating himself.

Again there was the faint sounds of a scuffle. Rye waited, resisting the impulse to hurry on ahead in the event Placido needed help.

"*Jefe,*" Placido's voice came quietly through the night. "It is well, but we must hurry. It is likely the woman will return."

"The Comanchero dead?" Dancy asked.

"It is so, *señor.*"

Rye glanced back over his shoulder to Ligon and the women, still crouched against the side of the corral. "Let's go."

At once they pulled away from the shadows, and following the lawman, hurried to where Placido was now waiting with the horses.

"Which way do we head, John?" Ligon asked as they helped the women to mount.

"South for a—"

"South!" Dancy echoed. "We better get away from this camp as fast as we can. I say we go north—"

"We will," Rye said, shaking his head, "but first we'll go south for a mile or so until we're well clear of this place, then we'll cut back till we hit the Rio Culebra. Can follow it north."

"That'll be a waste of time if you ask me," Dancy said and turned away. Ligon was struggling to get one of the women who seemed reluctant to mount her horse, into the saddle. The Ranger crossed to give his friend a hand.

One of the other women, the one who had taken possession of the rifle of the Comanchero killed back in the main house, hurried up to the scene of confusion.

"Dora—Dora," she said urgently, taking the woman by the hand, "listen to me. It's Arabella. We're leaving here, getting away from all those terrible outlaws. Do you hear me? We're leaving."

Dora allowed herself to be pushed into the saddle. "Leaving?"

"Yes, going away—going home," Arabella replied. "But you'll have to keep on being quiet. And you'll have to hang onto your saddle real tight so's not to fall off. We're going for a long ride."

Dora nodded absently. "Ride?" she repeated numbly.

"Yes, a long ride but when it's over you'll be home. Do you understand me?"

Dora nodded again. "I—I think I understand—"

Immediately Arabella wheeled and ran to her horse. Without waiting for assistance she put her foot in the stirrup and swung up into the saddle. Settling herself, she slid her rifle into the boot, and glanced about.

"We're all ready," she announced.

Ligon, going onto his bay, nodded to Rye. "We're all set, John. Best you lead the way."

"Still say we're doing this all wrong," Will Dancy muttered. "Ought to get as far from this—"

"Rye knows what he's doing, Will," Ligon said. "You just leave him be, let him run things."

"The Comancheros will not follow soon," Placido said, as the party moved off into the star-light-shot night. "The gates of the corral are open. Already the horses are wandering."

Rye grinned. "That ought to slow them down a mite for sure," he said. "Obliged to you for thinking of it, *amigo.*"

"*Por nada,*" Placido murmured as they rode on.

CHAPTER 14

Rye led the way due south, moving at a good but quiet pace, until they had reached a fairly deep arroyo well overgrown with brush. Riding down into it he changed course and followed the ragged cleft in a southeasterly direction until it flattened out and became a part of the vast mesa that lay to their right. At that point he cut a direct line for the river, now due west.

They moved fast and hard after leaving the brushy screen of the arroyo, and soon coming to the stream Rye called a halt to rest both the women and the horses.

"Why're we stopping here?" Dancy wanted to know. "Them Comancheros'll be coming after us mighty soon."

At that remark one of the women, Rye wasn't sure which but he assumed it was the one named Dora, began to weep.

"We'll be safe here for a bit," he said, glancing to the east. "Still a couple of hours before first light."

Dancy shrugged. "Somebody's sure to find them stiffs we left back there. And that woman—she's bound to go looking for her man. And don't forget about the one we left in the house, she could've got loose and—"

"She's been gagged and tied up good," Rye said.

"She won't be doing any hollering or getting loose on her own."

"You willing to guarantee that?" Dancy asked, his thick brows lifting.

"I guarantee it," Rye said flatly, keeping his temper in check.

"Well, I'm hoping you know what you're talking about, but you don't know them Comancheros like I do."

"Know their kind," Rye said coolly. "Anyway, we won't be here long. First thing I want done is to shorten the stirrups of the saddles the women are riding. They've got a lot of miles ahead of them and staying in the saddle's going to be important." He paused, put his attention on the women who had dismounted, walked down to the stream and were bathing their faces. "I doubt if any of them have done much riding."

"You're wrong there, mister," Arabella said, coming to her feet. As the others followed suit, she added, "I reckon we've all done our share."

Arabella was a large, well built woman in her late twenties or early thirties, Rye guessed. She had blue eyes, dark hair, and a firm, determined chin. Wearing a man's shirt and pants both sun-faded to a colorless gray, high button shoes, and a ragged straw hat, there was a toughness to her that declared her self-reliance.

"He's the marshal—U.S. Marshal John Rye," Ligon said frowning. "You can thank him for getting you and the others out of that hellhole."

Arabella smiled and nodded. "Sure am thanking him and the rest of you men, too. We'd about made up our minds that we'd be spending the rest of our lives in a—"

"Don't say it, Arabella," the youngest of the four women cut in. "I can't even bear to think of it."

She would be Ida Lee, the girl Dancy had said Hacho was taking such great care to preserve for one of his bawdy house customers. Young, with hair the color of a golden sunrise, pale blue eyes set wide apart in a beautiful face, she had a curvaceous, fully developed figure that the tattered brown dress she wore could not conceal. She had no hat but the shoes she had on looked fairly new.

"Don't say that, Arabella!" one of the other women mimicked. "Ida Lee, you've been hiding from facts ever since that filthy bunch of outlaws brought us in! Why, you haven't had it half as bad as the rest of us."

Rye, working at shortening the stirrups of the heavy Mexican saddle on the brown gelding that Arabella was riding, motioned to Ligon and Dancy.

"Let's get those other stirrups fixed."

Both men turned to do the lawman's bidding, Ligon doing so quickly, Will Dancy with less interest as if he felt the adjustments were unnecessary. Beyond him Placido was already at work removing the rawhide strings from the stirrup straps in order to shorten their lengths on the bay horse that the woman called Dora was riding.

There was a strangeness to Dora, a sort of emptiness, as if her mind no longer had any relation to reality brought about by some terrible scene or incident. Somewhere in her mid-twenties, she was clad in a filthy, once-yellow dress and run down black shoes. Her hair, dull from dust, was brown and the same color as her vacuous eyes.

"We going to eat here?" Dancy wanted to know, looking up from his chore. "Long as we're taking a chance doing this, we might as well go whole hog and do our eating."

Rye shook his head. "We'll do that later on, up the river."

He was growing a bit weary of the hostility in Will Dancy's attitude, and was doing his utmost to control his temper. The important thing in the marshal's mind now was to get the women back to the border and safely across the Rio Grande where they would be on American soil. Any differences he had with the Ranger had to be overlooked, or at least held in abeyance.

Myrtle, the last of the four women, was standing near Hugh Ligon watching him alter the lengths of the stirrups of the saddle on the white-legged black horse she was riding. Also somewhere in her twenties, she was a bit on the heavy side, had light colored brown hair and eyes, and a round, moonlike face that showed a deep sunburn from under the hat she was wearing. The calico dress that sagged limply on her frame was torn, and her shoes were coming apart, the uppers from the soles. At the moment she was speaking to Hugh Ligon in a low, confidential voice. The ex-Ranger appeared pleased at the attention she was paying him.

"Those outlaws—Comancheros you call them— what are they?" Arabella asked. "I never heard of them before."

She had addressed her question to Rye, now working on the saddle's second stirrup.

"He don't know nothing about them, lady," Dancy replied before the marshal could answer. "He's used to hauling in outlaws up in Kansas and places like that. Now me, I've been dealing with the Comancheros along the border for ten, eleven years."

Rye glanced at Arabella. A puzzled look was on her face. He grinned, shrugged. "I reckon he's right."

"You bet I'm right. Know them cutthroats first hand! This ain't the first time I've run up against them, no, sir, not by a bucket full!"

"Then maybe you can answer my question," Arabella said. "We were warned about hostile Indians when we decided to go west but nobody said anything about these—these Comancheros—whatever they are."

"They're mostly Mexican renegades," Dancy said. "Oh sure, there's a few Indians, Comanches and Apaches that run with them—"

"A few Americans, too," Ligon added. "Outlaws that've crossed the border to get away from the law."

Dancy frowned, spat, but he nodded. "That's right, but mostly they're Mexicans."

"Why do they call them Comancheros? That's an Indian tribe, isn't it?" Myrtle said.

"Yeh, the Comanches are a tribe. They call these renegade Mexicans Comancheros because they deal with the Comanche people."

Arabella hitched at her trousers. "Can't the Mexican government do something about them?"

"I reckon they try. The Mex government don't like them any better'n we do, but they're hard to run down. The army's on the lookout for them all the time but the Comancheros are too smart for them."

"Or too many," Ligon said. "We're always hearing about a party of *Federales* or *Rurales*—Mexican soldiers—being ambushed and killed by a bunch of Comancheros."

"Why doesn't the army just attack a place like where they were holding us captive?" Myrtle asked. "They could catch this Hacho and his whole bunch there together and wipe them out?"

The woman's voice had risen as she spoke, and her eyes hardened under her battered straw hat.

"They've tried—not only there at Vado but at other Comancheros' camps," Dancy said. "But they always get there too late. Somebody warned them and by the time the soldiers get there they're gone. Only people they find are old men and women who claim they don't know nothing about the Comancheros."

"Do you mean they protect the outlaws?"

"They're scared not to. If they done any talking about the Comancheros, admit they were there, or told where the outlaws had gone, they know they'll get themselves killed next time the Comancheros show up."

"And like as not get the whole village wiped out," Ligon said. "That's what happened to the one where Placido and his folks lived. One day they just rode in and killed off everybody in sight except for two young girls that they carried off. Ain't that right, Placido?"

Placido nodded. "It was as you say."

"He was off in the hills when they hit the village," Ligon explained. "Couldn't do nothing about it—but he's been killing off Comancheros ever since. I reckon you could say he has the right."

Arabella shook her head. "It must have been terrible for him."

"Can bet it was, but he never says much about it, just goes right along killing off a Comanchero whenever he gets the chance."

Myrtle stepped back as Ligon finished the job on her saddle. "Is that all the Comancheros do—ride around and rob and kill people traveling through the country?"

Will Dancy nodded. "That's about all. They trade the goods that're worth something to the Comanches, and sell the women to, well, to the bawdy houses in the big towns and the men to the mine owners. Lots of silver mines around here, and some gold."

"We were in Texas when they rode down on us," Arabella said. "Looks like the American government—our own soldiers would take a hand in stopping them."

"They have the same problem the Mexican's have: can never catch up with them," Dancy said. "About the only outfit that ever gets anything done are the Texas Rangers, but there just ain't enough of them—us."

"Are you a Texas Ranger?" Myrtle asked.

"Yep. Proud to say I am."

Rye finished with Arabella's horse. Ligon and Placido also were through with their respective tasks while Dancy had only to draw tight a final lacing. The marshal glanced at Dora. Her eyes were blank; her features devoid of expression. She was sitting on the remains of a log near the stream. It was apparent she had taken no interest in what had been said. Ida Lee, standing nearby, was listening but also had made no comment—actually had said little since they had first halted. Both Myrtle and Arabella seemed to resent her, probably because of the special treatment she had received from Hacho and the Comancheros.

"Let's move out," Rye said, turning his eyes to the east. It was still a couple of hours or so until dawn, until the time when Hacho and his outlaws would discover the escape of Will Dancy and the women, and the lawman wanted to have his party as far north from the Comanchero camp as possible by that time.

There was a short delay while the women climbed or were assisted up into their saddles and adjusted themselves to the shortened stirrups, but finally all was ready. Rye led the way across the narrow stream to the opposite side where he figured there was less chance of their being seen by any of the outlaws who would soon be searching for them, and then struck a course at a good pace along the river for the distant Rio Grande.

CHAPTER 15

If the situation had not been so critical, riding along the Culebra in the cool moon and starlight would have been most pleasant. The hushed desert had a pale, dream-like quality, and the faint rippling sounds of the river provided a lulling effect. Coyotes barked from a safe distance and their fiercer kin, the gray wolves, howled mournfully in the low hills to the west—small offsprings of the mighty Sierra Madre.

Rye kept the horses to a good, ground-covering pace. It was easy traveling and had the animals not been tired from previous use—especially those they had appropriated from the Comancheros—he would have pushed them much harder. Now and then he glanced back to reassure himself that the outlaws had not yet become aware of their absence and were now on their trail, but each time there was only the long, silvered emptiness of the night and the shadows of the brush and stunted trees that grew along the river to be seen.

"When are you aiming to pull up?" Ligon asked, kneeing his horse up beside Rye's big chestnut. "Them women ain't going to go much longer without resting."

Rye threw a glance to the east. The first pearl-like glare was showing beyond the horizon. It wouldn't be long until daylight and by then he had hoped not only to be well north of the Comanchero camp but also in an area where they could find adequate cover. He nodded to Ligon and turned his attention to the west, where a line of bluffs laid a dark outline in the growing light.

"Can pull up soon as we get there," he said, pointing to the irregular formation, and at once swung from the northerly course they had been pursuing, and headed for the bluffs.

Ligon dropped back to his place in the party, repeating the information the lawman had given him as he passed. Rye heard several murmured comments of relief from the women, but at once Will Dancy, drumming on his horse's ribs with his heels, hurried up to protest.

"Stopping will be a fool thing to do!" he shouted. "Them Comancheros will be on our tails by sunup —maybe already are. And they're good trackers. I say we best keep going."

"Can't get far on a dead horse," Rye said dryly, "and the ones we took from the Comancheros are pretty well used up."

"The hell—those horses can stand a lot of hard riding," Dancy scoffed. "They're used to it."

"Maybe, but they've had very little rest, and with a hot day coming on I've got my doubts they—"

"You don't know nothing about this country!"

Rye turned to Dancy. "What I do know is that with four women along I'm not taking any chances. It'd probably be all right if it was just you, Ligon, Placido and me, but that's not the way it is."

Rye turned his gaze to the east. The glare in the sky had strengthened and taken on a yellowish glow. Cactus and yucca plants were now starkly silhouetted against the growing light. He looked again to their back trail along the river. There was no sign of the outlaws, but it was still a good five miles to the bluffs. They would reach them before full daylight if they increased the pace. The lawman twisted about in his saddle.

"Got to hurry it up a bit," he called back to the lagging party dozing as their horses plodded woodenly along. "Going to be daylight in a few more minutes."

The horses broke into a slow trot and then a weary lope as their riders urged them on. The desert was flat and smooth and despite the occasional stretches of loose sand, and ragged, weedy mounds of rock, it was easy going. Wild things, encouraged by the coming day, were beginning to stir; doves, larks, and other birds took wing as they passed. A coyote, head and tail hanging low, cowered under a clump of greasewood, ignoring a long tail rat that scurried from one sun-blasted bit of grass to another as if seeking safe hiding, and high above it all, etched against the clear blue of the sky, several buzzards circled slowly as they scanned the land below for carrion.

When the party reached the first outcrop of broken country, Rye cut left and led the way down into a deep arroyo fronting the bluffs. The lawman did not halt immediately but continued on, wanting to put a distance between the point where he and the others would make camp and the place where they had turned off the trail in the event the outlaws tracked them. He was counting on the Comancheros assuming they had pressed on northward along the river; but as Dancy had noted, there would be trackers among the band of outlaws, and failing to catch sight of the escaped captives, they would resort to following the hoof prints of the *gringo*'s mounts, and eventually would discover where the party had turned west, and do likewise.

At a bend in the deep wash where brush grew thick along the floor and also overhung from the mesa above, Rye came to a halt.

"We'll be here all day," he said, dismounting. "Best you make yourself as comfortable as possible."

"Hard to do, this being the desert," Ligon commented. "I reckon we could stretch a blanket between them thorn bushes, make a sort of canopy for the women so's they could get out of the sun."

Rye nodded. "Be a good idea."

"Are we building a fire?" Myrtle asked. "I'm chilled to the bone."

The marshal shook his head. "Can't risk it. The Comancheros might spot the smoke."

"Hot meal sure would go good, specially some coffee," Dancy said, "but like Rye says, we better not take any chances."

Rye glanced at the Ranger. He couldn't recall their having agreed on anything prior to that point. There might have been something else, but if so it had escaped his mind. Whatever, he hoped the accord would continue; it was a long way to the border and they could expect the country in between to be alive with Comancheros searching for them.

While Ligon and Placido suspended a blanket between convenient brush clumps to ward off the coming brutal sun rays, and laid another beneath it for the women to rest on, Rye dug into his grub sack for food to make an early morning meal. It wouldn't be much, he knew; dry biscuits, jerky, and a can of peaches was all he could come up with. Bacon, potatoes, onions, coffee, and such that required a fire would have to wait for a time when there would be no danger from the outlaws.

"Best we go easy on the water," he said. "We've got three canteens all about half full."

"The river's not far from here," Arabella said, accepting the lawman's invitation to share his fare along with Will Dancy. "Could refill the containers—"

"There's a lot of open ground between here and there," Rye said. "If Hacho and his bunch are out looking for us—and they probably are by now—they'd spot somebody crossing over for sure."

"We can make out," Dancy said. "I'll wet a rag and swab the horses' mouths. That'll hold them till we get back to the river. Still be plenty for us."

The women had already taken shelter beneath the canopy Ligon and Placido had erected, and with the two men hunkered in the shade it cast, were laying out food from the grub sacks of Placido and the onetime Ranger. The sun was now well above the eastern horizon and making its presence felt.

"How long will it take us to get to the border?" Arabella asked.

"Five or six days, all depending on how much trouble we run into," Rye answered. "Expect we could do it in four if we traveled hard at night when it's cool—and didn't run into any of Hacho's cutthroats. Best we remember, however, they're better at finding us than we are at hiding from them. In the days to come we can't be too careful."

"*Jefe,*" Placido said quietly at the lawman's shoulder. "I go now."

Rye nodded and Placido rose and moved off down the arroyo at a slow run.

"Now, where's he going?" Dancy asked at once. "I never was one to trust his kind much."

"Felt that way myself at the start," Rye said, "but he's one you can bank on. He's going to where he can keep an eye on the trail along the river. He'll warn us in plenty of time if he spots any Comancheros coming this way."

"I reckon there ain't no reason why we can't grab a little shut-eye then," Ligon said, stretching out in the meager shade. "I can sure use it."

"We all had better get some rest," Rye said. "Once it's dark we'll pull out of here."

"You figure to go back to the river?" Dancy asked.

Rye nodded and settled back on one elbow. "Yes. We can stay out of sight better if we follow it."

"I don't know about that," the Ranger said. "This arroyo looks like it runs north. Could stay in it. Just might go for miles."

Rye shrugged. Dancy was back in form. "That's the problem—we don't know how far it runs. We do know the river goes all the way to the Rio Grande."

Ligon, full-length near the edge of the blanket on which the women rested, began to snore deeply. Arabella and Myrtle had lain back and closed their eyes, either sleeping also or simply taking their ease from the hot glare beyond the canopy. Ida Lee, having somehow come up with a small pocket comb, was running it through her yellow-gold tresses while on a back corner of the blanket Dora gently rocked back and forth singing in a low, quavery voice an old army song much favored by Confederate soldiers. Rye listened idly, having his own recollection of the doleful melody:

> *The years creep slowly by, Lorena,*
> *Snow is on the grass again.*
> *The sun's low in the sky, Lorena,*
> *And frost now gleams where flowers have been.*

It had been years since John Rye had heard the song, and always before it turned him thoughtful and a bit sad for it brought to mind the friends he'd fought side-by-side with in the war, and who he'd seen die. The conflict had been a waste of good men, but the leaders of clashing ideologies never seemed to realize that.

Rising, the marshal moved off up the big wash, restless and at loose ends with himself. If the war had been a waste could he say anything better about his own life? Since the war's end he had been a hunter of men, going through all the various phases as a sheriff, guard, outrider, deputy town marshal, bounty hunter, and in recent years a Special U.S. Marshal.

The Doomsday Marshal, they had come to call him. Armageddon personified, the finish, the end of life for those who had defied the law and for whom he had been sent to bring to justice—or kill if it became necessary. It was a grim reputation he bore, one accumulated through time, and one that he was never proud of, although, he had to admit, it did serve to intimidate and make his job easier.

"Going far?"

At the question Rye paused. It was Arabella. Despite present conditions and what she had endured in past days, or perhaps weeks, she looked rested and clean—evidence that she had likely used a portion of the drinking water allotted her to wash her face, neck, and arms.

The lawman shook his head. "Just didn't feel like sleeping," he said, pulling off his hat and brushing at the sweat on his forehead with the back of a hand.

"It was the same with me," Arabella agreed. "Too much excitement, I guess."

Excitement! Rye grinned at the word. It was a bit more than that! Hell, they were lucky to be alive— and the prospects of staying that way weren't all that good.

"Yes, I reckon it could be that," he murmured as they halted in the shadow of a stringy mesquite bending over the arroyo. The roots of the tree were partly exposed, a result of water rushing wildly down the wash at sometime in the past when one of the rare rainstorms lashed the land.

"I was watching you back there when Dora was singing," Arabella said, looking off across the desert. "The song meant something to you, didn't it?"

Rye nodded. "It meant the war, and friends getting killed—things like that. Heard the song many times when I was in bivouac."

"You were a Confederate?"

"Yes, in the cavalry. Joined up with Jenkins and rode with him until we went head-on against a big bunch of Yankees under General Crook. Jenkins was killed and a man named McCausland took over his command. Was with him for a time, then transferred to Nate Forrest's outfit."

A stiffness had come over Arabella. "McCausland," she repeated slowly. "The man who burnt down Chambersburg—"

"Was him. Happens I was with him at the time, in his cavalry. Can say it wasn't his idea; a general named Early gave the order and he was the kind of soldier who did what he was told."

Arabella shook her head. "That makes no difference. It was a terrible, cruel thing to do. I know, for I had family there, an aunt and uncle and several cousins. They all lost everything—the homes they'd put a lifetime into building."

"A lot of folks lost everything, not only in Chambersburg but all over the south as well as the north. That's what war's all about."

"Did you enjoy doing something like that?"

"No, I did what I was ordered to do—and far as war's concerned, there's nothing about it to like. Expect we better be getting back to camp. You'll need rest. We've got a long, hard night ahead of us."

The woman turned, and with the marshal at her side, started back down the arroyo. "I guess there's some excuse for your being a part of it. You couldn't have been much more than a boy when you joined the rebel army."

"Yes," the marshal said quietly, "along with a good many thousand others just like me who signed up to fight for what they thought was right."

CHAPTER 16

They moved out shortly after dark, striking off across the open flat for the river some distance to the east. Placido had maintained a watch on the trail paralleling the Culebra throughout the day, and while he had seen several parties of Comancheros moving along its winding course, all had failed to note where the escaping captives and their rescuers had turned off to hole up.

"Can eat a bite while we're riding," Rye had said, directing Ligon to pass around portions of their dwindling rations prior to the departure. "Later we can stop and—"

"If this is all the grub you've got," Dancy muttered, glancing about at the meager amounts of dry biscuits and jerky being allotted, "we're sure going to be starving before we get to the border."

"Aim to make what we've got last as long as we can," Ligon said.

What Dancy was overlooking was the fact that they had figured on four to feed, not eight, Rye thought, but he said nothing about it as no doubt it would make the women uncomfortable.

"There'll be rabbits along the river," he had said. "Probably berries and wild onions, too. We'll make out till we get where we're going."

"Just leave it up to Placido," Ligon had said

when he was finished distributing the food. And as he climbed up into his saddle, he added, "That man can scare up a meal on a rock slide if he has to."

They reached the Culebra without incident. Halting, they allowed the horses to rest briefly while they refilled the canteens and slaked their own thirst. When that was done, they permitted the horses to drink sparingly, as the animals had not yet cooled down completely; and then with Placido and Dancy leading the party and Rye and Ligon bringing up the rear, they rode on in the pale night for the border far to the north.

They held to that arrangement as they pressed steadily on. Rye had chosen to bring up the rear in order to keep an eye on their back trail, for he knew that pursuit from the outlaw camp would continue to come from that direction except, of course, if there were any of the Comancheros ahead and now returning. They, too, would follow the river and such could lead to a meeting head on, but the lawman was not too concerned about that; he was relying on Placido to give him ample warning if such developed.

They drew to a stop around midnight to let the all-important horses rest. The group took advantage of being out of the saddle to stretch and relieve their muscles. The women were suffering, Rye realized; all had done some riding but none were as accustomed to the saddle as was he and the other men. He could imagine the pain flogging their backs and legs as well as their shoulders from the long, hard ride. But there were no complaints from any of them.

With moonlight filtering through the few trees

and brush clumps along the river they rode on a half hour or so later. The desert to the west and east had come to life now that the piercing, hot rays of the sun no longer punished the land. The hot breath of the day had cooled and desert wild-flowers, primrose, Christmas cholla, datura with their white, velvety trumpet blossoms, and many other kinds were brightening the usual drag waste. An occasional rabbit, its cotton-tipped tail bobbing frantically as it rushed off into convenient brush, was seen. Doves, frightened by their hurried passage, fluttered off into the scanty growth.

"It's hard to realize a place can be so ugly by day and yet so beautiful at night—"

Rye, at that moment, was looking back to the trail they had covered reassuring himself there was still no pursuit by the outlaws. He came back around. It was Arabella. She had slowed the pace of her horse until she was alongside him. The hostility that had colored her tone earlier when they were speaking of Chambersburg and its destruction, was no longer evident in her voice.

"It's all of that for sure," the marshal agreed. They were moving at a fast walk, having reined in their mounts for a breather rather than pulling to a complete stop. "But don't ever underestimate the desert. It can kill you."

"Have you been here before?"

"On the desert, yes, but not this far down in Mexico."

"John," Hugh Ligon said, "I'm going to move up and ride with Myrtle for a spell. That all right with you?"

The lawman nodded. "Go ahead. Seems the Comancheros are doing their hunting for us in day-light."

"Sure looks that way," the ex-Ranger said, and spurring his horse into a trot, caught up with the woman he appeared to have become interested in.

"I think your partner there has taken a shine to Myrtle," Arabella said with a smile.

"He's a good man," Rye said noncommitally.

"I hope so. She's had it so hard. The family was on the way to Arizona—she, her father, mother, and two brothers—when the Comancheros attacked them. They were all killed but her. I'd like to see Myrtle end up with a good home someday."

"And you?"

Arabella turned to Rye. In the pale light her face looked soft and creamy beneath its tan, and her eyes appeared deep set.

"I don't know what I'll do, or where I'll go, I expect I'll have to find a job somewhere."

"What about your folks? Are they—"

"They were killed by the Comancheros, along with Ida Lee's family. We were in Texas, near the Quitman Mountains—I think I heard my pa call them—and had just made camp for the night. There were two wagons of us, the Briscoes—Ida Lee's people—my pa, me, and an uncle on Ma's side. We were about to eat supper when about two dozen of those murdering outlaws rode down on us. Hacho was their leader."

Arabella paused, stared straight ahead as if re-living the terrible moments of the attack.

"They killed everybody but Ida Lee and me—just shot them down—then took us and the wagons into Mexico and on to their camp. Somebody said there was a fort somewhere near to the Quitmans but we sure never saw it or got any help from the soldiers stationed there."

Rye shook his head. "I'm not familiar with that part of the country. Expect Ligon or Dancy could tell you—"

"Doesn't matter now—it's all over and done with. My only hope is that you can get us safely back to Texas. I'll make my plans for the future then."

"What about the other woman—the one you call Dora? I guess she lost her folks, too."

"I expect so," Arabella said, turning her attention into the direction of the Sierra Madre. The towering range of mountains appeared to reach up and pierce the dark sky above the flats spreading out from its base.

"I don't exactly know what happened to Dora and her family. Something terrible I'm sure because it left her mindless." The woman paused. A shiver shook her broad shoulders and she remained silent for several moments. Then: "I'm going to try and find a home for her, one of those places where they care for people like her—if we make it back to civilization."

Rye checked their back trail once again. There were still no signs of their being followed. "Don't worry too much about that—we'll get you there."

Arabella smiled, pulled her shawl more closely about her shoulders in an effort to ward off the night's chill.

"I expect if anybody can do it, it will be you," she said. "I remember your friend saying you are a U.S. Marshal."

Rye nodded. "Was in El Paso when Ligon asked me to help him get Dancy out of the Comancheros' hands. Known Hugh for quite a spell—and Dancy's a lawman so I couldn't say no."

"I see. Are you married? It must be very hard on your wife having you away on some dangerous—"

"I'm not married—and that's the big reason," Rye cut in. "I'd never put a woman I cared about through the worry my kind of job would cause."

Arabella shrugged, drew the shawl a bit tighter about her shoulders. "I think that would be something for her to decide, not you."

They rode on, shortly increasing the pace to a lope. Placido reported tracks of several horses, apparently Comancheros searching for them, but they had been made sometime the previous day, and were all leading south. Near daylight they approached a scatter of low hills, again to the west of the Culebra, and continuing to take advantage of the darkness, they crossed over and found a place in an area of ragged bluffs and buttes to make a camp —once again using a blanket for shelter from the sun.

"You reckon it'll be safe to build a fire?" Ligon asked after they had settled. "Placido killed four rabbits—hit them with rocks. We could all use a good meal."

Rye glanced to the sky. It was no longer completely clear. Dark clouds were piling up along the southern horizon and were spreading steadily across the gigantic blue arch. He nodded.

"Let's risk it. Scout up some dry wood so's there won't be a lot of smoke—and keep the fire small, just big enough to roast the rabbits and make coffee."

"Expect we best get it done soon, before the sun's up," Ligon said. "If those clouds keep moving in what smoke we do make ain't going to be noticeable."

"Just what I was thinking," Dancy said, and moving off along the wash began to collect fuel for the fire. Arabella turned to Rye.

"Myrtle and I—and Ida Lee will take over the cooking, if it's all right with you."

"Be fine," the lawman said. "The grubsack's are all yours. Not a lot left in them but—"

"We'll make do," the woman said and turned away.

She came to an abrupt halt as the warning buzz of a rattlesnake broke the hush of approaching day. Dancy, a few steps to one side of her, wheeled. Bending down he picked up an arm's length branch of dry, dead cholla. Again the rattler sounded a warning.

"Don't move!" the Ranger warned softly.

Stepping back slowly Dancy circled into the weed-covered, rocky ground beyond the serpent. The other women, Rye, Placido and Ligon—the latter with knife in hand ready to throw—watched in silence as the Ranger closed in with the cholla cane. It would have been easy to dispose of the rattler with a bullet but the sound of a gunshot no doubt would have far more dangerous repercussions than the snake presented.

Dancy, walking lightly, moved in on the reptile. The snake was now feeling the slight vibrations created by the Ranger's approach despite the care the man was taking and increased the intensity of its warning while its flat, triangular head and beady eyes drew back, ready to strike.

Abruptly Dancy reached out with the cane. He thrust it quickly into the coils of the serpent, and with a scooping motion, sent the snake writhing and twisting off into the rocks a dozen yards away.

Arabella gave a deep sigh of relief. Rye and the others relaxed and Hugh Ligon, sheathing his knife, said, "That sure was using your head, Will."

"You should've killed it!" Myrtle said, brushing at her face. "I—I hate snakes—and to think it was right here in our camp! Why, it could've bitten—"

"I guess you might say the rattler had more right being here than us," Dancy cut in with a shake of his head. "Out here we're the trespassers," he added and resumed his search for dry wood.

CHAPTER 17

They spent the hot, breathless day in the short hills
again sheltered from the sun by the blanket
stretched between brush clumps. Placido, seem-
ingly finding sleep unnecessary and constantly on
the prowl, kept watch for any Comancheros who,
unaccountably, had not as yet put in an appearance. But they were out there somewhere—of that
John Rye was certain.

They all rested much better that day, probably
because of better food and the simple fact they
were becoming accustomed to the way of things.
But on the next morning after camp had been made
a hundred yards or so west of the Culebra, Rye,
taking a long look at the river's course and the
country rolling out ahead of them saw that they
were now faced with a serious problem.

"What's the trouble, John?" Hugh Ligon asked,
noting the lawman's troubled countenance.

"We're running out of cover," Rye answered,
pointing. "The brush peters out a mile or so on."

"Long as we keep moving at night and hole up in
the day there ain't nobody going to spot us."

"Country north of here looks mostly bare and
flat. And with the moon bright like it is a party big
as ours could be seen for quite a ways."

"Yeh, expect you're right," Ligon said. The heat

was already building and sweat was shining on the man's leathery face. "You got something we can do figured out?"

Rye shook his head. "Not yet. Let's talk to Placido and Dancy."

Moving over to where the Ranger and Placido were hunched in the shade of a low bluff Rye outlined the problem. Dancy shrugged.

"Can't see as there's much we can do but chance it when we run out of cover."

"That would be the answer if there was just the four of us, but we've got others to think about. You both know this country better than I do. What about heading west for the Sierra Madre, then cutting north for the border?"

Dancy wagged his head. "Never'd get through that way. We'd run into too many soldiers. Hell, Chihuahua City's only fifty or sixty miles west. We'd not only have the Comancheros to worry about but the Mexican army as well."

Rye looked at Placido for confirmation of the Ranger's words. Placido nodded. "It is best we follow the Culebra. The danger will be less."

Will Dancy got to his feet and turned his attention to the north. He studied the country for a long minute and then shrugged.

"Well, I figure we've got about one more night that we can keep out of sight along the river. After that we'll be out in open country."

"Maybe something will turn up by then," Ligon said.

"Yeh, maybe," Rye said, "but we're in a country where we've got no friends so I wouldn't know who it might be. Once we reach the Rio Grande what's wrong with crossing over into Texas right there, and then heading north?"

"It's what folks call Lower Texas," Ligon said. "Got more Comancheros running loose there right now than you can stir with a stick."

Dancy nodded. "Reckon Hugh's right. Down there is where so many pilgrims get jumped. Best we stay out of that part of the country."

Rye swore softly and glanced to where the women, stretched out under the blanket canopy, were sleeping.

"I reckon there's nothing to do but keep on following the river."

Dancy shrugged. "It's the only answer—unless you figure Hacho's given up and ain't looking for us no longer."

"Not much chance of that," Ligon said, and looked at Placido. "What do you think, Breed? Has Hacho quit looking for us?"

"I do not think so, *señor*," Placido replied. "He will lose much face if he cannot find us and return us to Vado. It is a necessity that he do so—to show the people who follow him that he is a great leader and able to overcome all *Americanos*. Also, we have taken his prize—the women. That, too, must not be permitted to happen."

Rye brushed at the stubble beginning to darken on his face. They had no choice but to keep following the Culebra to where it met the Rio Grande, and there continue the same course, avoiding the open stretches where possible and taking advantage of every bit of available cover. By doing so—and with luck—they just might avoid an encounter with the search parties the Comanchero chief had sent out.

"Guess you could say we're in between a rock and a hard place," Dancy said with a tight grin as he settled back down in the rapidly disappearing shade of the bluff. Placido nodded to Rye and turning, struck off into the brush and rocks for a point where he could keep a watch on the trail beside the river. Ligon hawked, spat into the hot sand.

"John, I got something to tell you—"

"Go ahead."

"Myrtle and me—we've made up our minds to get hitched—married, soon as we get back to El Paso."

Rye smiled. "That's fine. Guess I ought to say congratulations. I'm glad something good's coming out of this for her, and you."

"Got my house and a little piece of ground where we'll live. Ain't much but we can get by—specially if I can get work now and then with Stoudenmire serving papers and delivering prisoners and the like."

"Expect he can keep you busy—"

"There's something else—we aim to take the girl, Ida Lee, in with us. She ain't got any relatives, and we ain't either. We'll sort of make a daughter out of her."

Rye nodded his approval. "She'll be needing a family."

"Kind of wish we could take in that other girl, the one called Dora, but we can only do so much."

"I don't think you need to feel bad about that. Arabella aims to look after her. She plans to find a home where she can be taken care of."

Ligon sighed in relief and spat again, this time against a nearby rock. The spittle sizzled noisily for a few seconds before drying up.

"What's Arabella going to do?" he asked.

"Figures to find herself a job—"

"We been wondering about you and her. Seen you doing a lot of yammering together, and she's kind of got sheep eyes for you. We thought maybe you two were getting lined up."

Rye shook his head. "She's a fine woman for sure, but I'm not in the market. You've been a lawman, and you know how hard this kind of living is on a woman."

"You ask her if it would matter?"

"Nope, and I don't intend to. Anyway, we better get them all back across the border before you or anybody else does any planning."

Rye turned to the blanket canopy. Arabella and Ida Lee were awake. Their attention was on Will Dancy who had trapped a scorpion in a small depression in the sand and was teasing the infuriated creature by blocking its every attempt to escape with a stick.

"This here's one of the real bad ones—the kind that can kill you," the Ranger was saying. "Can pick them out from the others by his yellow color, and that long, skinny tail. Them others hurt but they ain't killers."

Dancy continued to play with the scorpion which raced back and forth, jointed tail with its extended stinger curled over its horny body. Abruptly Dancy picked up a rock and ground the loathsome creature into the sand.

"I reckon that's that," the Ranger said, tossing

the stained rock off to one side. "Like somebody once said about the Comancheros—the only good ones are dead ones. The same goes for them poison varmints."

They passed that day resting and sleeping, and without incident. Late in the afternoon they ate sparingly of their limited stock of provisions and when darkness came, crossed over to the river and resumed the northward journey.

Near daylight Placido, scouting ahead as was his habit, returned. His dark sharp features were set to solemn lines.

"*Jefe,*" he said, pulling up before Rye when the party had halted. "*Soldados*—soldiers. They come this way."

CHAPTER 18

Rye glanced about. There was but little cover along the river at that particular point, but a dozen yards on a brushy draw cut away from the stream offering some protection.

"How many soldiers?" Ligon asked.

"They number fifteen, *señor*—"

Rye pointed at the draw. "That wash up ahead—looks like that's our best bet for staying out of sight."

Spurring the chestnut, the lawman led the way to the steep and narrow slash in the land. It was half-filled with weeds and other dry growth blown into it by the winds. Riding down into it, Rye turned to Placido.

"Are they out here on the flats or sticking close to the river?"

"They ride along the river, like we," Placido said. "With such heavy equipment they seek the coolness."

"Good," the lawman muttered. "If they'll stay over there our chances for not being seen in here are good. Keep moving. We best get as far back in the wash as we can."

"It flattens out about thirty feet ahead," Ligon, who was leading the way, called back in a low voice. "Ain't nothing after that but plain desert."

Rye looked to the river. A moment later he and the others came to a stop. In the pre-dawn light, and with the screen of intervening weeds and brush, however thin, the possibility of their being spotted by the Mexican cavalry was slim.

"Hunting for Comancheros," Dancy said. Like the others he was off his horse and crouched at the edge of the wash, attention riveted to the trail along the Culebra.

"If they're government soldiers and enemies of the Comancheros, why don't we join up with them?" Rye heard Myrtle say. "We'd be safer."

Dancy's reply was quick. "No we wouldn't. Be as bad off as if we got caught by the Comancheros."

"Why? If they're soldiers—"

"We're *gringos*—Americans—and we're not on good terms with the Mexicans. Could expect them to hand us the same treatment as they would the Comancheros."

Rye was only half listening, his attention being on the trail. The soldiers had rounded a bend in the Culebra and were now in view, riding loosely in no particular order. In the rising light their blue and red uniforms were in sharp contrast to their grayish background, and the buckles and other metal of their equipment glinted dully. Abruptly the man in the lead drew up in his saddle. He raised a gloved hand, and the patrol came to a halt.

"No talking," Rye said tersely. "He's looking this way. He's seen something that's got him suspicious —maybe one of our horses."

"They come over here we'll just have to fight it out with them," Dancy said. "Odds ain't good, but I can't see that we can do anything else."

"Stay quiet," Rye said. "Save your talking for later. He's not sure he's seen anything."

The officer turned in his saddle and said something to the man behind him. The soldier cut away from the rest of the patrol and rode leisurely toward the wash. One of the women stifled a gasp and Hugh Ligon, mopping at his face with his bandanna, drew his knife.

"Means a fight," Dancy murmured, squaring himself about and raising the rifle Ligon had lent him.

"Not yet," Rye cautioned. "Stay quiet. Don't move and don't be the one to start something. That soldier's tired. Probably been riding all night and he's half asleep. There's better than an even chance he'll never see us."

The marshal was right. The soldier, head low, rode up to within a dozen yards of the wash, and without looking up, swung his weary horse about and retraced his path to where the *Federales* waited. Reaching them he made a brief report to the officer in charge, after which the patrol moved on.

Rye kept his party in the depths of the brushy draw until the soldiers had rounded a bend in the Culebra and passed from view and then led them quickly back to the growth along the river. At once, Placido, at Rye's direction, struck off up stream.

"Could be another bunch around close," he explained. "I know you're all tired but there's no place to camp around here so we'd best keep moving."

"And moving damn fast," Dancy muttered.

Rye didn't wait for any other comments, either of approval or objection but, keeping an eye on the trail that alternately wound in and out of the brush, started north again. He wasn't certain what it was that pressed his mind and filled him with an urgency—certainly not the patrol of *Federalista* cavalrymen; they were well on their way in the opposite direction, but Rye had learned to never distrust the feeling and to take precautions no matter what the circumstances.

They rode steadily at a good pace for almost an hour, and then with the horses beginning to lag because of the difficult trail, they halted.

"Sure will be glad when we reach the Rio Grande," Ligon said as they dismounted. "Be easier—"

In that exact moment shots rang out and a half dozen riders—Comancheros—broke out of the thick growth, and firing as they came, charged down upon them. Bullets clipped through the leaves, all going wide of any target. It was evident Hacho wanted them all alive. The marshal reacted quickly.

"Get into the brush!" he shouted, drawing his gun. "And stay low!"

Evidently the outlaws had been following the soldiers looking for an opportunity to bypass and lay an ambush, Rye guessed, but coming upon him and his party, had switched their attention to them. That they were of Hacho's band was also evident as the big-hatted outlaw leading them was the Comanchero's second in command, Gatillo.

Rye, with echoing gunshots and powder smoke filling the early morning air, dropped to one knee and began to return the outlaw's fire. Ligon, Dancy, and Placido also opened up, and then a fifth gun close by him. He threw a hasty glance to his left, saw that it was Arabella. Holding her rifle steady, she was aiming, firing, and levering the weapon with cool regularity as the outlaws rushed toward them.

"Get this over fast!" Rye called out. "These shots are bound to be heard by those soldiers and bring them back."

"Can bet on it!" Ligon said, reloading his gun. "You women," he added, looking over his shoulder, "get down and stay down—real low."

One of the Comancheros, his dark, swarthy face set to hard lines, suddenly threw up his arms and fell from his saddle. Gunshots were a constant hammering now and the smoke, thin at first, hung in small, dense clouds throughout the brush. A rider appeared on Rye's left, his mouth wide open as he gave voice to a blood-chilling yell. The lawman snapped a shot at the hunched shape. The bullet missed as the outlaw swerved. In the next instant he had cut back and came directly at the marshal.

Gatillo! Rye twisted about for a better shot at the oncoming outlaw. In that same fraction of time Placido leaped out of the brush. A knife glittered in his hand as he dragged the Comanchero from his horse. Rye watched the knife rise and fall as it was being driven into the outlaw's body. Placido was having his moment of personal revenge.

The remaining Comancheros were circling in and out of the brush, firing and yelling as they whipped back and forth. Rye counted five. Evidently there had been seven on the party to start with—no doubt one of the several small posses

Hacho had sent to track them down. An outlaw crossed into a clearing on the lawman's right. Rye triggered a bullet and saw the man jolt and fall to the ground.

Arabella had apparently run out of ammunition as her gun was now silent, but farther over he could see Ligon, lying flat on the leaf-littered ground shooting with clock-like regularity at the weaving outlaws. Placido had now rejoined the party and was using his rifle. Rye saw two more of the outlaws fall. Three left, he thought, glancing about. Where was Will Dancy? He could see no sign of the Ranger.

Abruptly Rye was aware of a rider bearing down on him. Hastily pushing Arabella aside, he threw himself flat on his back. The Comanchero's horse was almost upon him with its rider leaning out of the saddle, dark face contorted, pistol pointed and ready to fire. At close quarters Rye triggered his sixgun. The outlaw's grimacing features disappeared in a mass of blood as the bullet met him head on.

Immediately the Comanchero's arms went around the neck of the horse as, reacting involuntarily, he struggled to stay in the saddle. The animal shied and leaped over Rye, came down solidly on all four feet. The impact jarred the man loose and sent him tumbling to the ground.

Ligon, on both knees, brought down another of the raiders. Blood showed on the sleeve of his shirt where a Comanchero bullet had found its mark, but judging from the man's actions, the wound was not serious. Rye drew himself partly erect in the hazy atmosphere and looked for the last of the outlaws.

He caught sight of the man just as Placido raised up out of the brush and shot him off the saddle.

A silence fell over the area broken only by the quiet sobbing of one of the women unnerved by the violence, and the diminishing sound of several of the Comanchero horses galloping off into the desert. Smoke and the acrid tang of gunpowder still filled the breathless air. Rye drew himself fully erect.

"Where's Dancy?" he asked, wrapping a bit of clean rag taken from his shirt pocket about the slight wound in his forearm where a bullet had cut a furrow.

"Over here, John," Ligon replied at once. "He's hurt bad. Took a slug in the chest."

The women began to rise as the lawman rushed to where Hugh Ligon was standing. Nearby Will lay on his back, a broad stain of blood covering his chest. The Ranger grinned weakly when he saw Rye.

"I reckon we showed them, eh, marshal?"

Rye knelt beside the man and pulled aside the sodden shirt for a look at the wound. Dancy had taken a bullet dead center. It was a miracle he was still alive.

"We sure did," Rye agreed. "Got them all."

"Like you said, them soldiers'll be coming back," Dancy murmured, his words slow and labored. "You best move on."

Rye nodded, and pulling off his bandanna, folded it into a pad, and pressed it against the Ranger's wound.

"I'll see to him," Myrtle said, dropping down beside the marshal.

"I reckon there ain't much use," Dancy said, as Rye started to rise. "Few things I need to say—"

"Sure, Will," Rye said, and turned to Ligon. "See if you and Breed can scare up some grub. Ought to be on the saddlebags of the Comancher—"

"Ain't but two of them still here," Ligon replied. "Others up and run off."

"Find what you can. Can use some ammunition, too. Arabella here ran out. Get the women to help —we don't have much time."

"Marshal, you best get going now—"

At Dancy's wavering voice Rye turned back to the Ranger. "We've got time."

"Before you go I want to say that I've been wrong about you. Know I'm cashing in so I want to get this off my mind."

"Forget it, Will—"

"No, it needs to be said. You—you're a top lawman. I was dead wrong about you. You're a lot better'n than I could ever hope to be. Expect that's what was bothering me—knowing down deep that was true."

"There's no need for all this, Will. I never—"

"The need is for me to get it off my chest," Dancy said, and grinned faintly at his own words. "I ain't got much of a chest left, I expect — now, I want you to move out, leave me be. We sure don't want them women ending up in the hands of them soldiers."

"You're right," Rye said. "We'll be on our way soon as we can load you up."

"Why bother?" Dancy said. "I'm done with living," he added, the words coming slowly from his slack lips. "You go on—leave me—"

Dancy's words halted abruptly. Rye looked more closely at the man. He was dead. Coming to his feet as Myrtle drew back, Rye crossed to the horses and took one of the blankets from the roll loosely tied behind the cantle of his saddle. As he started to retrace his steps to where the Ranger lay, Ligon called to him.

"Found a little grub—not much. And we got some cartridges that'll fit the rifles — How's Will doing?"

"He's dead," Rye answered. "Help me roll him in this blanket and load him on his horse, then we'll get out of here."

CHAPTER 19

With the help of Ligon and Placido, Dancy's stiff-
ening body was hung across the saddle of his horse
and secured. That done, the lawman turned his attention to the women.

"We don't know where that bunch of soldiers are
but I expect they're not far off. Means we've got to
get away from here fast."

The women began to climb up on their horses at
once, Ligon and Myrtle assisting Dora. Rye waited
until they were all settled and then mounted.

Squaring himself in the saddle he gave them a
quick look. He could forget traveling at anything
better than a fair pace. None of the women, with
the exception of Arabella, were accustomed to sitting a man's saddle, and chances were good that
before they got very far one of them—probably
Dora—would fall. That problem was further com-
plicated by having Will Dancy's dead body slung
over his horse, who made known its displeasure at
having a strange burden hanging crosswise on its
back by shying and rearing as Ligon took up its
lead rope.

But there was nothing to be done about any of it,
Rye realized. He'd simply have to make the best of
a bad situation. Moving out into the lead, he motioned for Placido to bring up the rear.

"Keep a sharp eye out for those *Federales,*" he said and urged his horse into forward motion. "If you catch sight of them, sing out."

"*Sí, jefe,*" Placido replied, and pulled aside to allow the women to fall in behind the marshal, after which Ligon, leading the horse carrying Will Dancy, pulled into line.

Rye set a good pace at once, keeping to the faint trail that followed along the west side of the river. He stayed close to the brush, sacrificing cover for speed as the horses could make much better time in the open where they were unhindered by the scraggly growth.

They rode until late in the morning, pushing the animals hard. The women, too, were suffering, not only from the saddle but the driving heat as well. Coming to a low, round-top butte rising near the river, Rye lifted his hand and signaled for a halt. At once, the women turned to the river, and quickly dismounting, refreshed themselves.

"It's hard going for them, John," Ligon said, also coming off his saddle. "Ought to go a bit easier on them," he added, a note of admonition on his voice.

"We slow down and we'll have that bunch of soldiers down on us," the lawman said sharply. "I aim to keep moving day and night till we get to the Rio Grande and cross over." Brushing at the sweat on his face, Rye turned to Placido, leading the horses to the water for a brief drink.

"Any sign of those *Federales?*"

Placido shook his head. "No, but they come."

Rye frowned. "Did you see dust?"

"*Sí, jefe,* twice. It is far behind, but they come."

The marshal, following Placido and the horses

down to the stream, pulled off his hat and ran fingers through his damp hair.

"We aiming to take Will's body clear back to Texas?" Ligon, standing nearby, asked. The man's face glinted with moisture and there were wet patches on his shirt where he had perspired freely. "He ain't got no relatives that I know of, and with them Mex soldiers dogging our tracks, I'm wondering if that's the best thing to do."

Placido was leading the horses away from the stream, having allowed them to drink sparingly. Arabella and the women were sitting on the low bank, feet in the water, while they wiped at their faces and other exposed parts of their bodies with wet cloths.

"If you're agreeable we can bury him here," Rye said. "Good place over there," he continued, pointing to a narrow but deep gully a few strides from the river.

Ligon gave it a moment's thought and then nodded. "Don't like leaving old Will down here in this godforsaken country, but I can't see as we've got any choice," he said, and taking the reins of Dancy's horse from Placido, led it over to the gully.

Rye followed and together they untied the blanket-wrapped body of the Ranger and lifted it off the saddle, after which they lowered it into the ravine. They had no tools with which to work, and improvised with sticks, loosening the soil on the sides of the gully and caving it in on Dancy's body. There were only a few rocks available, but with the help of the women who had come to attend the burial, they collected enough to lay on the top of the grave to further deter wild animals.

It was hot work and when they had finished both men were wringing wet with sweat. Together they returned to the river, and accompanied by the women, waded out into its shallow depth to spend a few minutes cooling off.

They spent a half hour allowing the horses to rest and have a second drink and then mounted up and rode on. They were drawing close to the point where the Culebra cut away from the Rio Grande, and again Rye considered the wisdom of crossing the larger river and entering lower Texas—dangerous country according to what he'd been told earlier.

"Hugh," he said later when they had again halted to rest, "you still think it's best we keep heading north and not crossing the Rio Grande here when this river comes to it?"

"Yes, sir," Ligon said in a positive voice. "Best we keep right on going up to the Rio when we get to it. Ain't nothing but trouble waiting for us if we cross over down here."

"Expect you forded up where Placido took me across. Lots of quicksand in that part of the river."

"Expect it's the same place."

"Well, I'll have to leave that all up to you and Placido," Rye said. "Sure'd hate to get this far and then run into a bunch of border soldiers."

"We won't," Ligon said confidently. "What I don't know about that neck of the woods, Breed does."

The marshal, satisfied they would be following the right course, turned to where the women were resting near the horses. Arabella had pushed her straw hat to the back of her head, exposing a wealth of chestnut-colored hair. Dora and Ida Lee now wore scarves in lieu of their missing headgear, he saw.

"I meant to ask," Arabella said as he took up the reins of his horse, "don't you want to say a few words over Will Dancy?"

"Can, if you like—"

"We could stop there by his grave for a few moments when we ride out—just out of respect. He was a brave man."

Rye nodded assent. "No doubt of that. He went through hell at the hands of the Comancheros."

Arabella was quite a woman, the lawman thought. She had stayed right in there in the middle of the shoot out with the outlaws, never flinching for an instant, and all the while matching their firing with her own until she had run out of cartridges. That would not happen again Rye noted, with a grin; the woman now had a full bandolero of ammunition slung across her shoulder.

They mounted up, rode slowly to the ravine where Dancy lay buried. For several minutes they sat in silence staring down at the rock-covered grave. Finally Hugh Ligon spoke.

"Will, we sure hate leaving you here but there ain't nothing else we can do because we're a far piece from the border, and getting you there, well, it would be a powerful chore.

"But we're wanting you to know we all are obliged to you for all you done, specially the ladies. If you hadn't spoke up about them we'd never known they was there, prisoners, and got them out. So, rest in peace, old friend, and like the Mexican folks say—*vaya con Dios.*"

Rye looked back over his shoulder. There was dust hanging in the cloudless sky beyond a bend in the Culebra, but so far no riders were in sight. They had a good start on the soldiers, he reckoned, but it would soon be lost unless they continued their hurried pace. He swung back around. Myrtle had dismounted and was placing a handful of yellow desert marigolds that she'd found near the river on the Ranger's grave.

"Let's move out," he said, and as the woman climbed back into her saddle, glanced down at the gully. Touching the brim of his hat he murmured, "So long, Will," and then rode on.

Spurring the chestnut to the head of the party, he put the horses to a slow lope, and once again staying along the scanty fringe of the brush growing along the stream, continued the ride for the border.

They stopped for rest around noon, resuming after a short time to halt once more three hours or so later. The sun was merciless and the horses had begun to wilt under the steady pace. All about them, except for the narrow strip through which the Culebra flowed, the land lay flat and barren, the only break being the mountains well to the west and east. Nothing appeared to move in the relentless heat except a broad-winged eagle soaring effortlessly high above them.

Rye had hoped to ride until dark, rest for a couple of hours and then push on. But the condition of the women and the horses forced him to call a halt well before sundown at a neck in the Culebra where a stand of mesquite offered a bit of dappled shade. Leaving Ligon in charge of the women and horses, Rye doubled back on foot with Placido to have a careful look at their back trail.

"Ought to be seeing that bunch of soldiers," he said as they climbed to the summit of a slight rise. After a bit he shook his head. "Nothing but a little dust."

Placido shrugged. "They ride in the brush close to the river. Also I think they are on the other side sometimes."

Rye gave that consideration. If the soldiers were doing as Placido said, it would account for their failure to gain as traveling would be slower, but it would be unwise to count on the *Federales* being delayed too much; they could decide to break out into the open any time and increase their pace.

Rye moved his party on within the hour, fully aware of the animals' poor condition—the result of having to survive on the scant, brown grass that grew along the river while maintaining a constant move for the border. The women, too, were worn and near exhaustion from the hard riding. Only Dora, sitting rigidly upright in her saddle, head tipped down, seemed unaffected by weariness as well as the danger they were fleeing.

They resumed their journey a short time later. Rye knew they could not go far but he felt that every mile counted and darkness would be their best ally. At full dark they came to a halt and made camp. They were all but out of food, but Placido again provided three small rabbits and a like number of doves, the former killed as they came out of their holes, the latter with a bit of looped cord at the end of a long stick.

"Will we be staying here till morning?" Arabella asked as they were preparing to eat.

The lawman shook his head. "Only until midnight."

Ligon looked up, a look of concern on his face barely visible in the low firelight. "I don't think these women can make it, John. They're just about all in."

The lawman shrugged. "I reckon they'll have to if they want to keep on living," he said, and walked off into the darkness.

CHAPTER 20

Around noon of the following day they reached the Rio Grande. There was not much difference in the growth along the larger stream at this particular point, it being somewhat barren, but Rye called a halt nevertheless.

"We'll be here an hour," he said as all but Dora dismounted.

Nodding to Arabella, who he noted was looking at him with a quiet smile on her lips, he started to turn away, but paused to watch as Ligon and Myrtle released a rope that tied Dora's feet to the stirrups and further secured her hands to the saddle horn. He had wondered at the woman's ability to stay on her horse during the more difficult areas of the trail. He realized now that Hugh and the women had taken means to see that such was possible.

They ate a quick lunch of dry biscuits, weak coffee and the last of the rabbits Placido had managed to provide. As Rye, empty peach tin serving as a cup from which he drank his portion of the brew in hand, made the rounds of the horses he was relieved to find that despite the hard going all were in fair condition.

The grain he'd brought along had run out, having been divided between the chestnut and the other horses. It had become nonexistent shortly after their leaving Vado and the animals had found grazing scarce. But now that they had reached the Rio Grande they would fare somewhat better as grass, while not thick and plentiful, was available. The lawman had been concerned about the horses and their ability to carry them all the way to the border, now he reckoned he—

"*Jefe*—"

At Placido's call Rye came about. He was standing a short distance from the thin shade, and hand cupped over his eyes to ward off the brilliant sunlight, was staring off into the south.

"What is it?" Rye asked, walking quickly over to the man.

"Soldiers come. Also there are others. Comancheros I think."

At that, Ligon, in company with Arabella, Myrtle, and Ida Lee, joined them. Rye threw his gaze down the long plain. Heat waves danced above the flat, scorched land, distorting his vision but after a few moments he was able to distinguish the *Federales*. The sun flashed and glinted against the metal parts of their equipment.

"Where are the others?" Ligon wondered. "I see the soldiers but I don't see nobody else."

Placido pointed off to their right. "Over there, *señor*."

Rye located them. A dozen riders coming from the direction of the low hills to the west.

"I see them now!" Arabella said. "It looks like they're planning to cut off the soldiers."

"Just what they're aiming to do, all right," Ligon agreed. "That'll sure get them off our tail."

"If they saw the soldiers, they saw us," Rye said. "That means they'll be coming after us if they get by the soldiers."

"Works both ways," Ligon said. "The *Federales* will keep on following us if they beat off them Comancheros."

"Which means we lose either way," Myrtle said in a hopeless voice.

"Don't give up," Ligon said hurriedly. "We ain't licked yet.

The Comancheros, apparently riding in an arroyo or similar low area that prevented the soldiers from seeing them, suddenly broke out into the open. Rye saw the *Federales* come to a halt and mill about uncertainly as the outlaws, in a cloud of rising dust, bore down on them. Surprise over with, they hurriedly strung out in a line and prepared to meet the attack.

"Are they some of Hacho's bunch?" Ligon asked, directing his question at Placido.

He nodded. "It is likely. All Comancheros in this part of the desert have joined with him. It could be Hacho himself."

It seemed likely to Rye. That the outlaw chief would have sent out several parties to search for them was only logical; they had seen signs of such. Now, with it becoming more apparent to the outlaw leader that the escape of his prize prisoners might be perfected, he no doubt had taken matters into his own hands.

The distant sounds of gunfire reached them, a hollow popping in the hot, dry air. Dust churned up by the hooves of the horses began to mix with powder smoke, and the distant scene became more obscure. Rye turned to the others. They had exchanged very few brief words with him since the previous night when, despite Ligon's plea to grant the women rest, he had forced them to ride on after only a short time. And now it would happen again.

"Best we forget resting up," he said. "We move out now we'll be able to keep a good lead on whichever one of them wins out."

"Yeh, I reckon so," Ligon said, agreeing. "Come on, ladies, time to go."

The women voiced no opposition, and shortly they rode on, maintaining a steady pace until dark when they halted in an arroyo a quarter mile or so from the river. They no longer heard any shooting and all wondered who had been victorious in the confrontation—but it really didn't matter; each knew that regardless, the winner would be bad for them should they be overtaken.

Around midnight Rye roused them and had them in the saddle again and on the move, and from that time on it became a series of brief stops followed by continual riding day and night as the lawman pushed steadily toward the border, and safety. Twice they saw riders in the long distance. That they were following them was clear, and that the horsemen were Comancheros was just as certain as there was no glinting of their equipment in the sunlight.

The horses began to lag on the fourth day, their strength fading under the punishing heat, and lack of rest and substantial feed. This, added to the lack of sufficient food began to tell on the women, and while none was near giving up, it was plain they had about given up hope. This was further heightened when the pursuing outlaws disappeared from sight—a fact that quickly increased their worry.

"They're out there, can bet on that," Rye said when Arabella wondered if the outlaws had turned back. "Like as not they're riding back in the brush close to the river where they won't be seen."

The women had more or less gotten over their hostility toward him, it evidently having become apparent to them that he was right and it was for their own good that he pushed them so relentlessly. Arabella had never really closed him out, and he was smiling at her when he had answered her question.

"Do you really think we'll make it to the border, to Texas?" she asked.

Rye shrugged. He was looking forward to night, to the time of darkness when he could lead the party off into the cooling desert, and finding a safe place, rest for a few hours. Although he made every effort to conceal it, weariness was weighting him down, too.

"Good chance," he said. "Just don't give up. The horses of the Comancheros can't be in any better shape than ours, and they're what's going to count from now on."

The woman considered his words thoughtfully. Then said, "Are we far from the border?"

Rye glanced about. "Only been through here once before, but I figure we're about one day shy of getting there."

Arabella brightened. "Then, if we can keep go-

ing, hold out that is, until tomorrow sometime
we'll be there?"

"I could be wrong but that's how I see it."

Arabella brushed at the sweat beading her face.
"I hope you're right—and I expect you are. I don't
think any of us can stand much more of what we've
been going through."

"Been tough," the lawman admitted. "Us being
where we are sort of proves what folks can stand
when they have no other choice."

The woman nodded, glanced at the rag around
his forearm. "Is that place where you got shot giving you any pain?"

"No. Wasn't much more than a scratch to start
with. I've been hurt worse falling off a horse."

Arabella smiled. "I can't imagine you ever falling
off a horse," she said. "I think you're the most com-
petent and bravest man I've ever met. I expect you
can handle any situation that might come up."

Rye shrugged, looked back over his shoulder.
"I'm not sure about that," he said.

Ligon and the other women were a few yards
behind him and Arabella. Placido, leading Will
Dancy's horse, was a short distance farther on.
There still were no signs of the outlaws. It would
be a great feeling to think they had turned back but
John Rye knew that was something he dare not as-
sume.

"I—I've been wanting to tell you something,"
Arabella continued.

Rye glanced at her. The blue of her eyes seemed
brighter than usual and her features were set and
calm.

"What?"

"It's about Chambersburg—some of the things I said."

"That was a long time ago," Rye murmured. "No need to keep hashing it over."

Arabella brushed at a wisp of hair straying down over her face. "I'm sorry if I sounded bitter toward you," she said. "I realized you were only doing what you were ordered to do."

"We all were," Rye said. "From the general on down. The whole thing was punitive—I think that's what they called it. Union soldiers had wiped out a southern town so the Confederate high command felt they had to do the same thing to a northern city."

"I know that—knew it all the time, but I still blamed the soldiers who took part in it. I just wouldn't admit to myself that you were all acting under orders. I'm sorry."

"Forget it. It's true that everybody loses in a war, regardless of who's right and who's wrong."

"I suppose so," Arabella said. "You keep looking back. Have you seen anything of the Comancheros?"

"Nope, nothing," the lawman replied as he turned his attention to the west. It was still an hour or so until sundown, and a couple more after that before full dark. "Be a while yet till it cools off some."

"I'll be glad when it does," the woman said, taking the front of her shirt near the collar and shaking it to release the heat trapped beneath the garment. "I never thought it could get so hot." She paused, looked around as Ligon, urging his horse to a trot, moved up beside the marshal.

"John, you aiming to stop soon?"

"After dark. Have to hold off a while yet."

Ligon shook his head, glanced at the sun. "Ain't sure the women, leastwise a couple of them, can last that long. Any chance we could pull up right now? Between the heat, all this riding, and nothing much to eat, they're about played out."

"I can understand that," Rye said, "but we're still up against the same problem—keep going or end up in the hands of Hacho and his bunch."

"I know what they'll all say to that choice," Arabella said at once. "They'll want to keep going even if they all have to be tied to their saddles. They—we—would rather die than become prisoners of the Comancheros again."

Ligon pulled off his hat. Like the others he had removed all unnecessary clothing, was dressed now in only pants, shirt, boots, neckerchief and headgear. His gray eyes appeared colorless in the deep red of his sun-burned face.

"I reckon we all feel that way," he said. "You seen any more of Hacho and his bunch?"

"No, not a thing," Rye answered.

"Do you suppose they've backed off and give it up? Maybe them soldiers hurt them plenty bad, and in this heat—"

"We don't know that, Hugh, and we'd be damned fools to take it for granted."

Ligon grinned wryly and replaced his hat. "Hell, I know that! Guess I wasn't thinking straight. Maybe the sun's getting to me."

"You can tell the women we'll pull up at dark, and if there's no sign of the outlaws, we'll stay put until daylight. That'll give everybody and the horses a chance to rest."

Ligon nodded approvingly. "That'll sure be good news," he said, and turning back, rejoined the women.

CHAPTER 21

Hot, dusty, and near exhaustion, they made camp near dark in the low hills that lay not far from the river. Rye could see no reason not to build a small fire for cooking as the Comancheros or the soldiers knew of their presence, if not their exact location. He felt that a hot meal—more rabbits, a squirrel, and again several doves provided by Placido as they made their way up the Rio Grande—was badly needed.

Too, the horses were in want of grass as well as rest and water, and after they had been picketed in a suitable place, and the women were occupied in preparing supper, Rye, in company with Ligon and Placido, walked a short distance in the fading day to a rise where they could view the surrounding country.

"I sure would like to know who came out on top in that little skirmish," Ligon said. Dust caked his sweat-stained clothing and rimmed his eyes and mouth. "If it boils down to a fight between them and us—and I get my druthers—I'll take squaring off against the soldiers."

Rye shook his head as he stared off across the desert, slowly coming to life. "We can't let it come to that. Any idea how far we are from the border?"

"Ain't sure," Ligon said, "but was I guessing I'd

say at least a day. You think that's about right, Placido?"

Placido shrugged his thin shoulders, and holding his rifle in crossed arms, dropped to a squat. His white duck pants were now a stained and dirty gray, his shirt was torn and hanging in shreds about his waist but the battered old army hat still sat at a jaunty angle on his head.

"It is for the horses to say, *señor*. One day if they are of strength, two if they are not."

Rye, also showing the ravages of the long, arduous journey on his bearded face and in the sweat-stained clothing he wore—now down to undershirt, pants, boots, hat and neckerchief, fixed his eyes on a thin smoke streamer well to the south.

"Is that about where the outlaws jumped the *Federales?*" he asked, pointing in the direction of the wisp of gray hanging in the clear sky.

"It'd be my guess," Ligon replied. "You reckon they've made camp for the night?"

Rye turned to Placido. "You know these people— do you think whoever won out—"

"It will be the Comancheros, *jefe*. They are much better at fighting than the *soldados*."

"And there was more of them, too," Ligon said, "leastwise at the start. Expect the *Federales* cut them down a mite, howsomever."

Rye finished his question. "What I'm wondering is, will they make camp for the night or keep after us? They know we're up ahead somewhere."

"Who can say?" Placido replied, his shoulders again stirring in the way of the Mexican people. "Perhaps they will rest, perhaps they will come."

Rye swore softly in exasperation. "What do you think they will do?"

"I would say they will rest the night. They have been much in the saddle, and there was also the fight with the *Federales*. Also, Hacho is a man with great confidence. He will believe that by resting his horses he can overtake us before the border is reached."

Rye smiled. "That's what I wanted to know. Means the chances are good that our horses, and us, can get a good night's rest."

"Well, we sure can use it," Ligon said. "Soon as I'm done eating I aim to go over to the river and just plain fall in, wash off all this dust and sweat—and cool myself down."

"Might suggest that to the women, too. Expect they would feel a lot better if they could clean up."

"I'll tell them," Ligon said, and started back down the short slope for the camp.

"We best not just take it for granted that Hacho and his bunch won't move out tonight," Rye said as he and Placido turned to follow the ex-Ranger. "They could fool us so we'll plan on standing watch, each of us doing about three hours."

Ligon hesitated. "Then you're figuring to pull out early—before sunup—"

"Right—"

They continued on, reached the camp. The women had crumbled the last biscuit into Rye's frying pan, added a small onion chopped to bits, a potato also cut into thin pieces, both which they had found in Ligon's grub sack, a quantity of water, pieces of a rabbit left over from the noonday meal, and had a stew under way.

On a second fire they had begun to roast the squirrel and the rabbits along with the doves. And on a flat rock placed near the flames they had laid out the tortillas found earlier in the saddlebags of the Comancheros they had encountered. Placido dug into his own near empty grub sack and contributed what remained of his corn cakes.

"Smells like a mighty fine supper coming up," Rye said, hunching down beside Arabella.

She looked up from stirring the stew. "There won't be much of this, and we've worn out the coffee grounds," she said, "but I guess you could say it'll be better than nothing."

Myrtle, turning the sticks on which the meat was broiling, made a wry face. "I never thought the day would come when I'd get sick of eating rabbit—but it sure has. When we get back to civilization I never want to see another piece as long as I live!"

Ida Lee, shifting the tortillas and corn cakes about on the hot rocks in order to warm them thoroughly, smiled faintly. "And bread," she said. "I'd give a lot for a piece of light bread."

"Don't fret," Ligon said. "It won't be long until we'll be back where we can get all we want to eat. Placido figures we can make it in a day—maybe a little more."

Arabella again put her attention on John Rye. She was frowning. "I guess that's how long it will take if we don't have more trouble with the Mexican soldiers or the Comancheros. I noticed you looking off in the direction of where they were doing all that fighting. Do you think they will be coming soon?"

The lawman saw the women, with the exception

of Dora, pause and wait for his reply. Over along the river, a dove was cooing plaintively and somewhere in the distance a coyote began to bark.

"We'll be all right until morning."

"Morning!" Myrtle echoed with a sigh of relief. "That'll give us a chance to rest."

"And clean up," Ligon added. "We can all go over to the river and wash off."

Rye was aware of Arabella's steady gaze still upon him. "You're not too sure of any of this, are you?"

The lawman shrugged. "Can't be dead sure of anything. I'm hoping we can all get a night's rest—same for the horses, but if it looks like Hacho and his bunch are on the move earlier than we're figuring, then we'll have to pull out, too."

"How will you know?"

"Aim to keep watch. Ligon, Placido and I will take turns at—"

"I can stand guard," the woman said at once. "So can Myrtle."

"It won't be necessary. Best you and the others see to it that you're ready to ride at short notice in case we spot the Comancheros on the move."

Arabella resumed stirring the stew. "Don't worry, we'll be ready," she said quietly.

Rye drew the first watch, Placido the second, and Ligon the last. Arabella once more endeavored to persuade the lawman to allow her and Myrtle to share the vigil, but as before, he refused, believing that if it came down to a hard, continuing race for the border the following day, or the next, the women should be in the best possible condition.

Rye found it difficult to sleep. After an hour or

so, restless and filled with uneasiness, he rose, made his way to where Ligon was perched on the crest of the rise they had earlier used to search the desert for signs of the outlaws.

"It's Rye," the lawman called softly into the darkness. Clouds had lifted during the evening and early part of the night, hiding the moon and stars to some extent.

"I'm all right if you're coming to see if I'm on the job," Ligon replied, rising.

"Not it. Just plain can't sleep. You see anything suspicious?"

"Nope," Ligon said. "So dang dark out there a man couldn't spot a hay wagon coming at him."

Rye stared off into the gray distance. There was something wrong—something wasn't the way it should be. It had kept him awake, troubled him ceaselessly, and while he couldn't put his finger on it, he took it as some kind of warning and refused to ignore it.

"We're moving out," he said abruptly, and started back for the camp.

"Why? You see something?" Ligon said, his voice filled with bewilderment as he followed.

"No, just got a feeling that we'd better pull out."

"You think them Comancheros are up to something, pulling a trick, maybe?"

"Could be—and we're not about to wait around to find out."

Ligon nodded vigorously. "Amen to that!"

They reached the camp and immediately aroused the women. Placido, evidently sensing something was wrong, scrambled from the clearing toward Rye.

"There is trouble, *jefe?*"

"Not yet," the lawman replied, "but I've got a hunch that it's on the way. We're moving out soon as we can get ready."

"I will go see—"

Rye shook his head. "No point—and I'd rather have you with us in case they've somehow got ahead of us and aim to cut us off from the border."

"It will be as you say," Placido murmured, and wheeling, padded silently off to get his horse.

The lawman turned his attention to the others. Dora was in the saddle, her feet already affixed to the stirrups and hands to the saddle horn by Myrtle and Ligon. Ida Lee, too, was mounted, and Arabella, having gotten the remaining horses, was waiting nearby. Her features were calm, but pale, in the dim light as she faced the marshal.

"Are they close?"

Rye frowned. "I don't know where they are—and maybe I'm wrong. I've just got a feeling we'd best get away from here." Reaching out he took the reins of the chestnut from her. "I'm obliged to you."

"I reckon we're all ready," Ligon said, coming up at that moment.

Gathering up the lines of his and Myrtle's horses, he led them to the edge of the camp, assisted the woman to mount and then swung up into his own saddle. Arabella was on her brown before the lawman could offer to help, and so climbing up onto the big gelding he spurred out to where he would be in the lead of the party. Placido, he noticed, was now riding the Comanchero horse that

Will Dancy had used, leaving his own to follow along unattended.

"If we get split up," Rye said, "just keep going north—up the river. You'll come to the border."

Without waiting for any questions or comments, the marshal cut about and following the trail that ran close to the brush, set a fast pace. It could all be unnecessary inasmuch as immediate danger from the outlaws was concerned, but there was no way to be sure.

They rode on steadily while the desert gradually brightened despite the overhanging clouds. Rain would be welcome, Rye thought, but he had his doubts that it would come. Birds began to make their presence known in the growth along the river and somewhere along its twisting course ducks were quacking noisily as they fed in one of the numerous backwaters.

Sunrise was a blazing band of color along the eastern horizon that faded swiftly into a gray haze, but it brightened the land and brought into focus the gaunt cholla cactus, agave plants and various other yuccas that in the night appeared so mysterious and grotesque.

"*Jefe—*"

The marshal reined in his horse as Placido galloped up and halted at his side.

"The Comancheros?" he asked, knowing the answer before it was voiced.

"*Sí.* I count the number of nine."

Rye swung the chestnut about and threw his glance to the south. Nine riders. Their leader was on a pure white horse. They were coming up fast.

"It is Hacho," Placido said. "He rides the white horse."

CHAPTER 22

Ida Lee began to weep brokenly. Myrtle kneed her horse over to the side of the girl, and leaning over did the best she could to put her arm about Ida Lee in an effort to comfort and reassure her.

"They ain't got us yet," Ligon said grimly, and glanced at Rye. "What had we best do, marshal—try to hide in the brush along the river or keep running?"

"We keep going," Rye answered. "There's not enough thick brush along here to cover us. Now, I want you to take the women and head out fast. Placido and I will follow."

"Country's looking a mite more familiar," Ligon said, glancing about. "Don't think it's as far to the border as we figured. Come on, ladies—you heard the man!"

They moved out at once, the horses breaking into a fast trot and then a good lope. Someone had gotten through to Dora and warned her anew to keep both hands clamped about the big horn of the Mexican saddle she was sitting.

They rode hard for a good hour. Rye, with Placido close by, continually kept a close eye on the Comancheros. The outlaws had not gained on them but as the miles wore by and the horses began to slow, the lawman could see the distance separating them gradually narrow. He looked ahead. A fairly high rise lay not too far away. It would further tire and slow the horses. Rye turned his attention to the river. It offered little if any protection. They had no choice but to keep going and hope that when the Comancheros caught up it would be in a place where he and the others could make a stand.

They reached the top of the rise with the horses blowing hard and covered with sweat. Off to their left a shallow swale, where trapped rain water collected during the infrequent storms that visited the country, provided a fertile area for mesquite, chaparral and other desert shrubs to flourish.

"Keep going!" he shouted to Ligon as he slowed the chestnut.

The ex-Ranger hesitated and then nodded as he understood what the marshal had in mind. He pointed ahead to a dark line on the horizon and to a thin cloud of smoke rising beyond it.

"That'll be the border—"

Rye nodded. The point where they would cross the Rio Grande and be in Texas appeared only five or six miles away but he knew that in the clean air distorted by heat waves distance often was deceiving.

"Get the women to it!" the lawman called back. "We'll stall Hacho and his bunch as long as we can, then we'll catch up."

Ligon nodded in understanding, yelled something to the women at which they started down the slope at a run. With Placido close by, Rye cut around, his attention again on the outlaws now coming up fast. He shifted his eyes to Placido. The man's face was a study in pure hatred as he, too, watched the approaching Comancheros.

"This way!" he yelled to Placido.

Continuing on north down the far slope of the rise as if to continue with Ligon and the women, he instead veered left when they were below the crest of the hill and rode into the brush-filled swale. He knew that he and Placido could expect little protection from the thin, ragged growth in the hollow, but it might afford an element of surprise and enable them to slow Hacho and his men for a few precious minutes.

Jaw set, Rye watched the Comancheros drive hard for the base of the rise. Hacho, bent low over the white horse he was riding, was in the lead while his men both flanked and followed close behind.

"*Jefe,*" Placido called above the faint pounding of the approaching horses. They had dismounted quickly and were now crouched in the rank growth. "I will ask of you a great favor."

"Name it," Rye answered. The lawman had drawn his .45 and had it in hand. His rifle, placed on a low embankment before him, was also ready for use.

"Hacho—I wish for him to be mine. I wish to be the one who takes his life."

"It's jake with me," the marshal said, "but I doubt we get to do much choosing. The odds aren't exactly in our favor."

With the ratio nine to two his words were hardly an exaggeration, Rye thought grimly, but a man in his line of work could never be certain of what he was up against; he simply went ahead and did the best he could with whatever fate and lady luck threw at him.

"*Buena suerte, jefe,*" Placido said. "It has been a great honor to know you."

Rye nodded. "I think what you said was good luck. Same to you—on both counts."

The lawman crouched lower. Hacho and his men had reached the base of the rise. Dust was spinning up from the horses' hooves, and the shine of sweat was on the intent features of the riders.

"Let them get about halfway up the slope," Rye said in a taut voice, "then start shooting."

Placido's reply was low, almost inaudible. "*Sí, jefe,* I will wait."

The lawman, sixgun in hand, hammer at full cock, drew a bead on the nearest outlaw. It would be easy to single out Hacho as the Comanchero leader was slightly ahead of his men, but he would respect Placido's wish to settle with him. It was a matter of personal vengeance, and it was only right that Placido's desire be granted.

He looked down the slope. The Comancheros were at the midway point. To let them get any closer could result in he and Placido being overrun.

"Now!" he said in a firm voice, and pressed off a shot.

As the Comanchero he had singled out buckled and fell from his horse, Rye heard the blast of Placido's rifle. Hacho flinched. His horse began to curve left—straight toward the swale. The remaining outlaws, momentarily confused, began to veer into the opposite direction. Evidently they were not certain where the two shots had come from.

Rye snapped a bullet at another Comanchero and

saw him fall. The outlaws, over their surprise, began to wheel away into a circle, firing as they rode through the shifting dust. Rye cursed as a slug drove into his leg. Missing the bone, it passed entirely through. Grabbing his bandanna, he wrapped it about the wound. From the corner of an eye he saw Placido go down.

In the same breath of time he heard a horse pound up from behind them—from the north. Rye half turned, his first thought being that one of the outlaws had circled around to their rear. Surprise rocked him; it was no Comanchero—it was Arabella.

She left the saddle on a run, stumbled, went to her knees. Up at once, rifle clutched in her right hand, bandolero swinging from a shoulder, she raced on. Breathless, she dropped down beside Rye, busy reloading his handgun.

"Looks like you could use some help," she said with a tight smile.

Arabella did not wait for a reply but began to fire at the outlaws, circling the swale much as a party of hostile Indians attacked a wagon train. Rye saw her hesitate as the outlaw she had caught in her sights through the smoke and dust haze, fell from his horse.

"Good shooting," he said, recognizing the vacuum-like pause that sometimes claims a person who has killed for the first time. "We're cutting the odds."

Arabella moved her head numbly, and then, as if getting control of herself, resumed firing her rifle.

Rye flinched as a bullet sliced a burning path across his forearm in almost the same place he'd been hit when they had encountered Gatillo and the outlaws with him. Ignoring the stinging wound, he continued firing. There were still four or five Comancheros left—it was difficult to tell exactly which. Hacho was down, was now hunkered behind a clump of chaparral engaged in a gun duel with Placido. He was dragging one leg, had left the low embankment in the swale and was crawling toward the Comanchero chief, firing as he painfully made his way toward the outlaw.

"Placido!" Arabella yelled suddenly. "Look out!"

Rye swung his attention hastily back to the right. One of the Comancheros was bearing down on Placido at full gallop. Instantly Rye rolled to his back. Taking quick aim he triggered his weapon. The outlaw threw up his arms, twisted about and fell from his running horse but not until Placido had taken another bullet from his rifle—this time in the back.

Placido faltered only briefly, and then still dragging his useless leg, blood now staining his shirt from the collar down, continued to crawl.

"Keep the others off him!" Rye shouted above the thud of horses' hooves and the crack of rifles as he snapped a shot at one of the riders swinging in close. "He's got a score to settle with Hacho!"

Arabella nodded, made a reply inaudible to Rye. She was hunched on her knees thumbing cartridges from the belt looped over her shoulder as she reloaded her weapon. Dust and sweat streaked her face, and her dark hair had come loose and was now hanging about her shoulders.

"How many more of them are there out there?" she asked.

"Not sure," Rye answered. "Hard to see. Maybe two or three." He shifted his eyes to Placido, who was almost to where Hacho, evidently sorely wounded, was lying.

In that next moment the outlaw leader drew himself partially erect. Through the drifting pall Rye saw the outlaw raise his rifle. The marshal started to warn Placido, but Placido had seen. His rifle spoke at the same instant as that of Hacho. Both men jolted from the impact of the heavy caliber bullets finding their mark. Hacho sank back, became partly hidden, but after a few seconds Placido, only a half dozen strides from the outlaw, resumed his slow, agonizing approach.

"There goes one of them—getting away!" Arabella yelled, and raising her weapon leveled a shot at the departing Comanchero. The bullet missed but apparently came close as the outlaw, big hat off and held to the back of his head by the chin cord, crouched lower and began to rake the sides of his horse more vigorously.

"Damn!" Rye heard the woman say feelingly. "I—"

"*Asesino!*"

Placido's high, wild voice carried to Rye through the hovering gray and tan pall. "*Asesino!*"

The marshal saw Placido's arm raise. A knife glittered in his hand as he threw himself on the outlaw chief. A muffled gunshot sounded. Placido rose slightly as a bullet, fired at close quarters, drove into his lean body, but his arm continued to rise and fall as hate guided the blade clutched in his hand and plunged it time after time into the outlaw.

Fascinated, Arabella stared at Placido. "What is—"

"Hacho killed his ma and pa, and carried off his two young sisters," the lawman said. "Don't fault him for what he did."

Arabella, on her feet, shuddered slightly. "I—I can understand. Do you think he's dead?"

Rye, reloading his half-empty sixgun, slid it into its holster and got to his feet. There was no need for it now; with the exception of the one who had escaped, the Comancheros were all dead. Limping badly, he crossed to the chaparral where the two men lay. Placido, the upper part of his body and one leg crusted with drying blood, sprawled half across the outlaw. Hacho's dusty shape was also stained by darkening red from bullet wounds as well as a dozen knife thrusts.

Arabella was silent as Rye lifted the body of Placido off that of the outlaw and then shook her head.

"I was taught to never speak ill of the dead, but I'm glad Hacho's been killed. He's where he'll never harm another woman—or man—again."

Rye shrugged. "Good riddance for sure. Only thing is there's always another like him to take over. Maybe that one that got away."

Arabella brushed at the perspiration on her dirt- and dust-marked face with a bandanna taken from the back pocket of her pants.

"I suppose so. Can only hope that if he does he'll soon run into another party of men like you and Placido, and the other two, Ligon and Dancy — You're hurt. I want you to sit down and let me take care of those bullet wounds before you do anything else."

Rye needed no persuasion. The place in his thigh was paining intensely and the furrow in his forearm still smarted.

"Have you got any medicine—anything to—"

"In my saddlebags," he replied, lowering his pants to where she could get at the bullet hole. "There's some rags and a can of antiseptic."

Arabella procured the items, bringing with them his canteen of water. Wetting one of the rags she washed the wound, applied antiseptic and then finished the treatment with a bandage.

"I'll take care of your arm now," she said.

"Can let it go," the lawman replied, starting to rise. "Just nicked me—"

"Makes no difference—it bled. And long as I've got the medicine out, I might as well doctor it—you sure don't want it to mortify."

"Not much chance of that," the marshal said, "but go ahead.

"Sure want to thank you for coming back and lending Placido and me a hand," he said when she had completed tending to both of the minor wounds. "You showed up right when it counted most."

Arabella smiled at him. "I couldn't bear thinking of you two having to hold off the Comancheros alone."

Rye glanced about as he got gingerly to his feet. The horses, tethered to a stand of mesquite a short distance below the hollow, now that the shooting and wild riding of the Comancheros was over, were standing head down and slack hipped in the driving sunlight.

"Are we going to bury Placido out here like we did Will Dancy?" Arabella asked, as with the lawman, she crossed to the waiting mounts.

Rye shook his head. "Nope. Aim to load him up on his horse and take him home to his wife. I figure he's got that coming to him."

CHAPTER 23

Late in the day with the heavens to the west ablaze with color, they reached the Rio Grande below El Paso. Having taken the same path that Placido had followed in the beginning, Rye, with Arabella at his side, and trailing the horse bearing Placido's body, waited for an opportune moment when there were no border guards around and then quickly led the way across the river onto Texas soil.

"I reckon we've made it," the marshal said, drawing to a halt when they were on solid ground. He shifted on the saddle; his leg pained considerably, but going to a doctor about it would have to wait.

"I'm—I'm so grateful to you," the woman said, sighing deeply. "I doubt if we'd ever gotten through it all alive if you hadn't been with us."

Rye shook his head. "I had plenty of good help," he said, and added, "That includes you. If you hadn't come back I expect I'd probably be laying out there with those Comancheros, stone dead. Let's take Placido home, then we can go to the hotel."

Arabella nodded. "And you can see the doctor about your leg." She had said very little since the shootout with Hacho and his men, either shocked by the violence and killing, or so weary that her senses were paralyzed.

Unexpectedly she began to speak, her voice high and ragged. "I hate this country! I hate every inch of it—the heat, the desert, the cruelty that's a part of it! I can't see how anyone in their right mind can stand to live here."

Rye raised his eyes to watch a flock of crows straggling across the sky toward the big cottonwoods growing in the valley west of the settlement where they would roost that night.

"You get used to it," he said.

"I don't think I ever could!" Arabella declared. "I want to be in a big town, a place where there's stores, and you have neighbors, and folks dress up —and you don't ever have to be afraid of things like outlaws and rattlesnakes and scorpions." She paused as the horses plodded wearily on in the yellow glow of the fading day. "Do you live around here?"

Rye had loosened his money belt and taken out two gold double eagles that he intended to slip in Placido's pocket before he turned the body over to the man's wife.

"No, I don't live anywhere permanent. I'm on the move most of the time," he said, buttoning the pocket of the belt and pushing it back into place.

"I see. Where are you from originally?"

"Tennessee. I guess you could say the nearest place to a home I have is in Kansas—a town called Wichita. I sort of headquarter out of there."

"Will you be going there next?"

The lawman stirred again on his saddle, seeking more comfort. The crows were gone and his attention was now on a coyote slinking through the brush off to their right. He'd not shaved in days

and his hard cornered face was covered with a dark
field of whiskers that made his slate blue eyes appear lighter. That effect was heightened by the hair
coming out from under his flat-crowned, plains-
man-style hat, and curled about his ears and down
over his neck.

Dust caked his sweat-stained clothing, but despite the weariness that gripped him, there was no
indication of such. He still looked the tough, lethal,
utterly controlled man that had earned him the by-
name of Doomsday Marshal, the dreaded lawman
of the frontier.

"I never know what my orders will be till I see
them," he said. "Could be word from the chief marshal waiting for me at the sheriff's office in El Paso.
If not, I aim to ride on to Wichita."

"Wichita," Arabella echoed, her voice rising. Because of the heat, so intense along the river below
El Paso, she had removed the bandolero with its
loops of brass cartridges, and hung it on the over-
size horn of her saddle. "Is it a big place?"

"I guess you could say so—"

"Then—could I go there—ride with you?"

Rye made no answer. The prospect of having a
woman companion on the long journey to Kansas
did not especially appeal to him; it would not only
slow him down, but present many complications.
He straightened slightly. Just ahead through the
trees and brush he saw the clearing where Placido
and his family lived, and veered toward it.

Immediately Placido's children came running
out of the house as they approached. All halted
abruptly when they saw the body hanging across
the saddle of the horse trailing the marshal. A mo-

ment later Placido's wife appeared. She hesitated briefly in the low doorway and then came out into the yard, sprinkled and swept to a hard surface consistency. Again she paused, her expression unchanging when she saw her husband. It was as if she had expected him to meet death during one of his journeys into the country across the border, and thus was not surprised.

Rye dismounted, brushed aside the blanket covering Placido and slipped the double eagles into his pants pocket. Then, removing the ropes that bound the body to the saddle, he lifted the slight, bloodstained figure and carried it into the house—no more than a single, large room with bunk-like beds, stove, shelving cluttered with pans and foodstuff, table, and several small benches. The walls were bare except for some clothing hanging from pegs near the doorway, and for a crucifix that looked down upon it all from above one of the windows.

"I'm sorry," the lawman said as he laid the lifeless body on one of the beds. "He was a brave man."

He didn't know if the woman understood or not. It would be up to Hugh Ligon to explain what had taken place, which could come about only after he had told of the showdown with Hacho and his men.

"Ligon will come see you," he said, and nodding to the cluster of silent, dark-eyed children, returned to where Arabella waited with his horse.

"It didn't seem to affect her," Arabella said as he mounted and they swung back onto the trail. "I mean the fact that her husband has been killed."

"Sometimes it takes a while for it to sink in," Rye

said. "Expect we can find Ligon and the women at the hotel."

Arabella nodded. "They're probably wondering if we're still alive." She hesitated, bit at her lower lip. "You never answered my question. Can I go with you when you go on to Wichita? I don't want to beg, but—"

"Not sure yet what I'll be doing — There's the town up ahead. The hotel's off to the right."

In silence they rode up to the hitch rack of the hostelry. As they climbed down from their saddles, Ligon, with Myrtle and Ida Lee, and a tall young man wearing a star, hurried out to meet them.

"John!" Ligon shouted, as he hurried up with extended hand. "Been watching for you—and we'd about give you up."

Rye grinned. "Been a long day—"

"I'll bet it has. I was aiming to scare up a couple of men and go after you if you all hadn't showed up by dark. Where's Placido? He go on home?"

"He's dead. We took his body over to his place."

"Oh, hell," Ligon said in a falling voice. "I sure hate to hear that. How'd it happen?"

Rye glanced at the women, embracing each other and plying Arabella with questions. "He fought it out with Hacho. Asked me to do him that favor. Was a sort of shootout and hand-to-hand duel. Both died."

Ligon nodded slowly. "I reckon that's just what he wanted. He lived for one thing—making Hacho pay for murdering his family. What about the rest of the Comancheros?"

"One got away. Arabella and I were able to take care of the rest. Is there a doctor around here somewheres? Hole in my leg needs looking at. Then I've got to go see the marshal, find out if he's got a message for me."

"The doctor's office is right by the hotel," Ligon replied. He turned to the tall man with the star. "Been so busy talking I plumb forgot to introduce you. This here's Dan Clark. He's one of Stoudenmire's deputies. He's got a letter for you."

Rye swore softly. A letter could mean that his hoped-for ride to Wichita was out, that he was being dispatched to some other town where his services were needed. Running a thumb under the seal of the folded sheet of paper, he opened it. He swore again. It was from the chief marshal. Fort Worth—in Texas. He was to go there, take charge of a killer who had been sentenced to hang in a Nebraska town, but escaped. Rye was to return the outlaw for execution.

"What is it?"

Arabella had turned away from the other two women and was watching him closely, a hopeful look in her eyes.

"Orders from the chief marshal. I'm to go to Fort Worth, then to Nebraska."

"Fort Worth, where's it?"

"Right here in Texas," Ligon said. "Pretty nice town."

Arabella took a step closer to him. "Then—can I —will you let me—"

"Up to you, but you'll have to stay in Fort Worth. Taking you on to Nebraska would be too risky— for you."

Arabella smiled. "Fort Worth sounds good to me. When do we leave?"

"Couple of days. Need to let the doc fix me up so's I can ride easy—and you'll be needing some rest and some good meals—"

"You all could come out to my place, only there just ain't room," Ligon said. "I—"

"Hotel'll do fine," the lawman said. "You send word to the Rangers about Dancy?"

"Had Stoudenmire do it first thing," Ligon said.

John Rye glanced about. The day was losing out to night and a slight coolness was setting in. It was good to be back in civilization—better yet to be alive.

"I reckon that takes care of it," he said. "I'll see you later at the hotel," he added to Arabella. "Right now I'm going to pay that doctor a visit."

THE MAN BEHIND
THE BOOK

"I appreciate my readers' loyalty. I've tried to never let them down with a second-rate story—and I won't."

No Western author has been more faithful to his fans than Robert Raymond Hogan, a man known as Mr. Western by Old West fans in over 100 countries around the world. Since the appearance of *Ex-Marshal* (1956), his first Western novel, Ray Hogan has produced entertaining Western stories of consistent quality and historical significance at a breakneck pace.

This prolific author's credentials rank him among the great Western writers of all time. Hogan's credits include 145 novels, and over 225 articles and short stories. His works have been filmed, televised, and translated into nineteen foreign languages.

"I'm a person with a great love for the American West, and respect for the people who developed it. I don't think we give enough credit to the pioneers who moved west of the Missouri in the early days."

Ray Hogan's ancestors first arrived in America from Northern Ireland in 1810. Commencing with his great-grandfather who journeyed from Pennsylvania to Kansas around 1825, losing his life to Osage or Pawnee Indians, the Hogan family history is one of western migration. His grandfather moved from Tennessee to Missouri, and his father began a law enforcement career as an early Western marshal in the Show-Me State before moving to New Mexico when Ray was five years old.

The wild frontier of yesterday is simply family to Ray Hogan. His lawman father met and talked with Frank James after the famous outlaw was released from jail, and once suffered a serious stab wound in the chest while bringing a train robber to justice. Ray's wife, Lois Easterday Clayton, is the daughter of a New Mexico family with its own pioneer heritage. Her grandfather began commuting between New Mexico and Missouri by horseback and stage in 1872 as a circuit-riding Methodist preacher "with a rifle across his knees." At one time he encountered the Dalton gang in Missouri.

Ray Hogan's boyhood was spent hunting, fishing, and riding horses in the New Mexico backcountry; observing all that was said and done on working ranches; and cocking an ear in hotel lobbies while railroad men, rodeo performers, townsmen, and cowhands talked about life on the range. It was only natural he decided to devote his lifetime to firsthand examination of the Old West.

Ray Hogan is a meticulous researcher, his investigations having taken him all over the West. An extensive personal library of books, pamphlets, maps, pictures, and miscellaneous data attest to his ravenous appetite for Western details. Throughout his intense, lifelong study he has painstakingly strived for authenticity.

Readers equate a Ray Hogan Western with excellence. His trademark is a good story full of human interest and action set against a factual Western background.

"I've attempted to capture the courage and bravery of those men and women that lived out West, and the dangers and problems they had to overcome."

Ray Hogan still resides in The Land of Enchantment with his equally talented wife, Lois, an accomplished artist and designer. This outstanding American continues to deliver in a way unsurpassed by his peers, keeping the Old West alive for those of us who missed it.

WITH'